TRUDI WITHOUT SIMON

(Trudi sans Simon)

Chapter 1.

When Nicole told me of Simon's death, at 2 pm., the 16th January, I thought I was going to die myself. I staggered in the corridor outside my bedroom, our bedroom, the conjugal bedroom Simon and I had occupied for such a short time. I thought I was going to be sick. Her whispered, 'Trudi I am so sorry, I have to tell you that Simon,' (I looked her in the face, thinking she would say that he had been detained by the police but instead she continued), 'he died in hospital this morning.'

I re-entered the bedroom, Nicole following behind me and I sat on the dressing stool, my face crumpling into tear stained ugliness. A sharp pain mounted in my forehead and another in my throat as I tried to stifle my sobs. I turned away from the dressing table mirror, not wanting to see myself. Even Nicole's arms about me seemed an encumbrance, although she, for the very best of reasons, just wanted to somehow comfort me in my intense grief and I knew she too, shared my shock and hurt. She let a sob escape. For I know not how long, we clung to each other like lovers, sobbing together.

At last, I managed a husky, 'How?'

'Une crise cardiaque. A heart attack.'

Simon, my Simon, my heart did not want to believe what my head knew to be true. Nicole did not lie or joke about such things. She was my right hand, my tried and tested assistant. I had parted from Simon at the hospital, just hours

Also By Adrienne Nash.
'Trudi'
'Trudi in Paris'
'Trudi and Simon'

<u>Crime Novels</u>
'The Cellar'
'A Time to be Brave'

Art. as 'Adrienne May'.

'Wide Skies', a history of art in Norfolk and of the Norfolk and Norwich Art Circle, 1885 to 2003. With statistics by Brian Watts.

ago, where he had been taken after a heart attack in the police station. The night before I had pleaded for his release to no avail. Now he was dead.

'Where and how did he die?' I managed to ask at last.

'In the intensive care. That is all I know.'

How would I live without the person who had virtually made me? Simon had paid for my surgery, supported me financially and sheltered me After the death of his wife, we had lived together and married, all in a period of less than six years. I could think of nothing except the gulf left by his death. Poor Nicole could not help me, no one could. No one could bring him back and I did not know how I could go on without him.

'Nicole,' I said, as soon as my throat was under enough control, 'can you leave me please. Help Sophie. Take my phone and keep it and yours handy, in case there are any messages. If you can't deal with it, ask them to call later or take a message.'

She did as I asked. When I was alone, I threw myself on the bed and sobbed under the duvet, not wishing anyone to hear. It did no good. There was no release from the emptiness of my life without him. Gradually my mind came round to thinking of what I would have to do. Simon would have expected me to be strong as I had always appeared to be, but he did not know how often I had quaked inside as I pretended strength. There were questions I would have to ask. What had happened while he was in custody? Why had he died in intensive care?

We had been together such a short time, married just over six months officially. Pictures of that glorious wedding day came into my mind; of nearly stumbling as I entered the Basilique and Nicole holding me up; and of Simon's strong grip on me as I walked down the aisle after the ceremony; of tears in my father's eyes and my brother in his dress uniform, all navy blue and gold and the red band around his cap, his sword at his side. Simon, so gentle with me all the day, and so charming to my friends and relations.

I gagged and thought I should be sick. I caught my breath and used all my self-control to stop the howl that tried so hard to escape from its cage within my diaphragm. Slowly I gathered my strength and recovered my breathing. Simon, Simon I breathed as though I could bring him back.

I raised myself and looked out of the window onto the calm Parisian street lined with plain trees, my vision distorted with tears. The trees were bare of leaf in this month of January, but their trunks are still fascinatingly mottled. They had been pruned, ready for the spring still three months away. A watery sun appeared from behind clouds sending a beam of light into this old fashioned Parisian bedroom. Nothing had changed except that my Simon, my beloved husband and master, my creator and benefactor was no more. I had become so dependent on him that it was like a pronouncement of death upon myself.

The silence was oppressive. A scooter roared momentarily, a long way off and was gone, leaving more silence. I could not stand the absence of any sound to anchor me in this World. I selected a disc for the player, Roxette, a disc from school days. 'It must have been Love', started to play:-

Lay a whisper on my pillow, leave the winter on the ground.

I wake up lonely, there's air of silence in the bedroom and all around.

Touch me now, I close my eyes and dream away.

It must have been love but it's over now. It must have been good but I lost it somehow.

It must have been love but it's over now.

From the moment we touched 'til the time had run out.

Make-believing we're together, that I'm sheltered by your heart.

But in and outside I've turned to water like a teardrop in your palm.

And it's a hard winter's day, I dream away.

I listened to the plaintive words, a parallel to my emotions and thoughts and I sobbed and choked anew. I looked at my tear stained face in the mirror. I cleaned the scant makeup from my skin, now smudged and tear stained and began afresh. When I finished, I did not look well, but better than ten minutes before. I went to the wardrobe, wondering what a young widow should wear. At times like this, I had always relied on Simon to select my clothes and often to dress me, pleased to be his mannequin. Today, from now on, I would have to make my own decisions. I chose a black and white dress, which accentuated my figure with shoes to match and a black heavily embroidered jacket. I did my hair carefully, classically, putting it up, pinning it, making it neat and tidy. I clipped in the last wisp of hair and surveyed the result. I looked cool, crisp and neat, an ice queen in the great European tradition. I had to be the ice cool blonde, Grace Kelly, controlled, beautifully presented. I needed to be what Simon liked and expected me to be.

Today, I could not be Scarlet O'Hara from 'Gone with the Wind', my fictional heroine who in times of stress would say, 'I can't think about that now, tomorrow is another day'. This time I had to take command and attend to the worst of things, the death of my beloved husband at the absurdly young age of thirty-nine. I am a widow aged not yet twenty-four.

I found Nicole in the nursery where she was playing with the children and assisting her sister Sophie, our nanny. No, my nanny. Neither of them knew what to say, except, 'je suis désolé Trudi'. What else was there to say? I too was desolate. They both hugged me and the children, not understanding, joined the group hug.

'Now it is all about these little ones. They are my future now.'

'You know we will do anything, Trudi.' Nicole said.

'Merci,' I whispered. 'Nicole, will you drive me to the hospital please, now. Sophie, I do not know what time we will return, but you can look after the little ones, can't you? I want you both to know that everything remains the same, except that Simon is not here.'

At the hospital we made for Professeur Rousse's office. I knocked his door and awaited his invitation to enter. There being no reply, I entered to find no one there. We went to the desk and the duty nurse told us that Rousse was on his ward rounds. She informed me that Simon's body now lay in the morgue. I phoned Sabine.

'Sabine, I have some really bad news. Simon died in hospital this morning and I need your help.'

There was a silent pause.

'Sabine?'

'Trudi. How? When?'

'Today. The police were questioning him again last night and he had another crise cardiaque. I am at the hospital. Sabine, listen, can you inform everyone there, but first, before that, will you please arrange for an undertaker to collect his body from the morgue at Pitié Salpêtrière. Yes, local from your area, your father may know someone. I will try to arrange the funeral in Lisieux. Thank you Sabine. Oh and phone Wally too, wherever he is. Merci Sabine. No not now, I will explain all later.'

That done I phoned the Maison and asked for Jacques.

'Jacques, I have bad news. It is not easy to say, a terrible shock. Simon est mort. I know, I do not know how to say it gently. If I did then I would collapse. I have to be strong, for everyone. It is breaking my heart, but we think of the future, yes? I want you to please inform everyone, including Annette. Yes, Nicole is with me here, she will be with me all today and probably for the rest of the week. She can work from home too. Yes, we will be making a press announcement. Of course, everyone will attend the funeral, I hope in Lisieux. Coaches yes. Thank you Jacques. I hope to see you all soon.'

After that we sat waiting for Rousse.

'Nicole, can you please arrange a press release. Just that it is with deep regret we announce the death of Simon Chartrand, Comte de Beauvonne and owner of Maison Beauvonne, in the Pitié Salpêtrière from un crise cardiaque. The funeral will be announced at a later date. Is that all right Nicole. Nothing we should add?'

'No Trudi. It is the curse of Beauvonne, but I think the newspapers will pick up on that.'

'Oh yes, I suspect you are right. We should give his age too. Thirty-nine. Could you do that now, phone the Press Agency. You don't mind staying with me do you?'

'Of course not Trudi, that is what I am here for.'

'Thank you Nicole, thank you so much.'

Rousse appeared as Nicole went to phone the news agencies. For the first time, he welcomed me with a kiss, took my hand and propelled me towards his office. We seated ourselves.

'I think I told you when you last sat in this office, that his heart was not in good condition. We had repaired the valve but we could not repair the damage to the muscle. I had thought that leading a less stressful life, he would have managed for some time before we had to think about a transplant. One never quite knows. I am so sorry Trudi.

'Oui maitre. Thank you, but it has been a terrible shock even so.' I could not control myself and found it impossible to speak. I started to cry again while Rousse sat his side of the desk. He put out a hand and held mine in a grip so strong that it seemed to drain the emotional pain. Gradually I regained control. I took two or three deep breaths and managed to speak again. 'I am arranging for collection of the body. I do not understand these things. Will there have to be a post mortem or can I ask them to remove him immediately?'

'You may make arrangements Trudi. It is enough that he died in hospital under my care from a known defect, so no post mortem. What are *you* going to do. You will need time away from your study?'

'Oui maitre. I need to take six months off at least. It was Simon's dying wish that I follow my dream and become a doctor, but at the moment, I have too much to do, a business to run, the estate and three little children who need a mother as well as a nanny. Is it possible to take time out?'

'I understand entirely Trudi. Yes of course. I will speak to the authorities and they will make it official. Do not worry and keep in touch with me.'

'Merci Maitre. I hope the funeral will be in Lisieux. I would like you to come and Professeur Deraveau too. Do you think that possible?'

'For myself, I will be privileged. Deraveau will have to answer for himself.'

'Thank you so much Maitre. I have much to do and so do you. Thank you for your kindness.'

'May I say, Trudi, you are very much a lady. I wish you bonne chance and I hope to welcome you back in time.'

We kissed and I left him at his door. I could feel his eyes on me as I walked away. I collected Nicole.

'I have made the press release Trudi. Anything else?'

'No, I just have to see Deraveau. Then we go to Lisieux. Can you find the phone number for the Basilique while I speak to him please?'

Deraveau was very busy, but I managed to have a quick word. Surprisingly, he was quite emotional. He cuddled me in his bearlike arms, held my face in his soft hands and looked deep into my eyes. 'You take care, and come back when you are ready.'

So that was all right. Nicole and I were soon in her small Mercedes and on the way to Lisieux. I phoned the Basilque and spoke to Abbé Thomas, outlining what had happened and making an appointment, but because of events there, he could not see me until the morning. I arranged a meeting for 11.30.

'Change of plan Nicole. Take me to the police station please.'

When Nicole had parked, I phoned mother.

'Maman,' I said, using the French term, 'Mum. I have some bad news.'

'What have you done now?'

'No not me. Mummy, it is Simon. I have to tell you, he has...... died. He was in hospital, another heart attack.'

'Oh Trudi, that is so unfair. As though your life has not been difficult enough. I am so sorry. Does that mean you are coming home?'

'No mother. This is my home now. I have three children, the business and the estate to run. Of course not. Do you not realise, I have lost the man I love. The man that did so much for me.'

'Of course dear. I'm sorry, I was just thinking of you. It is difficult to understand that you are, were married, let alone now a widow. It seems such a short time that you were just, little.'

'Mother, I can't do everything from here. I would like you to inform the family.'

'Yes dear, we will do that. Do you want to speak to your father.'

'Non Maman, I have too much to do. I will phone again tomorrow. Bye.'

Poor mother. I don't think she yet got me but then she never really had. She had gone along with my girliness, but only because it seemed to be a fait accompli having realised that I would not have made much of a boy or a man.

We entered the police station. An officer stood at the desk. I asked for Alain Barre or Olivier Roux, the officers who had questioned me and kept Simon needlessly in a cell where he had fallen ill.

'Madame, they are busy. Can I help?'

'Perhaps. Tell them that I have come for the possessions of Simon Chartrand. Tell them also that I shall be bringing a case for wrongful arrest and causing his death. Tell them now.'

'But they are interviewing a suspect at the moment Madame.'

'Then interrupt, I am sure they will want to know.' He looked straight at me, disconcerted, then cast his eyes down and disappeared behind a screen. I could hear muffled conversation.

He reappeared. 'I will see whether they are available Madame.'

I stood waiting. I did not like to sit in that place amongst the flotsam of Parisian society

In a surprisingly short time Barre appeared looking disconcerted.

'Madame, will you come somewhere private?' I followed him into an empty interview room, Nicole at my heels. We all seated ourselves.

'You have something to say to me that is this urgent?'

'Oui Monsieur Barre. Firstly, I want my husband's possessions, which I presume are still here, though he has died in hospital.' He looked surprised. 'Oh did you not know?'

'Non Madame. Je suis désolé.'

'Non, Monsieur, je suis désolé. I warned you that he was an ill man. It was in your power to release him but you chose not to. He fell ill, alone in his cell under your jurisdiction. I want his personal belongings, now Monsieur.'

'They are already finding them Madame.'

'Monsieur it is probable that I shall sue you for causing his death. I warned you he was not a well man, yet you kept him here. There was absolutely no reason to, on the word of a dead fool? I will drag you through the court Monsieur and your career will be over.'

'Madame, I implore you to be reasonable. I was merely doing my duty.'

'Non Monsieur. I asked you to be reasonable and you were not. Now it is my turn to be unreasonable. Actually, I do not care whether they find you guilty or not, but the case will ruin you one way or another.......' An officer appeared by his side with a plastic bag of Simon's possessions, keys, a handkerchief, a little change and his wallet, phone and a pen.

I signed a form.

'Madame, I am truly sorry for your loss. I could not know that Monsieur would fall ill. I beg you to reconsider.'

'My mind is made up Monsieur Barre.' I almost spat the name. 'I think you heavy handed. You had a duty but you could have been reasonable. It was as though you were determined to get my husband one way or another. You hunted and harried him Monsieur. And while alone in your cell and unable to communicate he had another heart attack. You say that you could not know he would feel ill, yet I specifically informed you that he had a heart condition. You gambled with his life, as though it was a personal vendetta. I am going to harass you Monsieur, for taking him from us. I bid you bon soir. Come Nicole.'

Outside we entered the car. 'Trudi, be careful. He can make trouble. Will you really take him to court?'

'I do not know Nicole. I am just angry, I am so hurt and angry. I want to hurt someone. I miss him so Nicole. I don't know how I can go on without him.' My throat hurt again as I fought back the sobs. When I recovered I said, 'Nicole, I cannot go home at the moment. Will you drive us to Willi's and we will have dinner, please.'

'Of course Trudi. I understand.'

'Thank you Nicole. You know you are like a sister to me. Thank you so much.'

'Moi aussi Trudi.'

Willi's was full, but Nicole spoke to the Maitre d' and we were found a good table. The place was really buzzing. A girl sat at the bar, singing and playing the guitar, somehow being heard above the buzz of conversation and clinking of cutlery and glasses. It was a cheerful, delightfully Parisian scene, fashionable people drinking and dining, the girl singing.

I asked what Nicole would like to drink and she reminded me that she was driving. 'We can take a taxi, leave the car here.'

'Non Trudi. I will not drink. For me, just a juice.'

'Very well, you are right. I am having a Firefly.'

'What is that?'

'Vodka, grapefruit juice and grenadine. A double.'

The waiter took the order. We looked at the menu. I needed something plain, good. We both decided to have fillet steak and chips.

'Trudi, are you really going to take the police to court?'

'I really don't know. But I don't see what trouble he can make. I have done nothing illegal. Beauvonne has done nothing illegal as far as I know. What I know is that Simon is dead. I cannot bear the thought of him in that cell, alone and unable to get help. Oh you remind me, I have to speak to the lawyer.'

I searched in my bag for Antoinette Dupois' card. I phoned her.

'Antoinette, c'est Trudi Chartrand. You are aware that Simon has died? Non? The police have not told you?'

'Non Trudi . They just told me this morning that he had been taken ill and was in hospital. They said that you were informed. What happened?'

I explained, managing to control my emotions. I explained also what I had said to Barre, threatening him with a court case for damages.

'I am so sorry Trudi. I will think about suing. What else would you like me to do?'

'Obviously, I need to see Simon's will, and soon. He may have left directions for his funeral etc. I am proposing to have it at Basilique de Lisieux, but he may have other wishes. I also need to know my position, my legal position. It was his wish that I should be the children's mother, but of course I do not know the legal position and there is the business and the estate. Can I see someone at eight tomorrow morning? I already have other appointments and have to be in Lisieux at eleven thirty, though I could put that off.

'Trudi I will meet you at the office at eight and I will have an associate there to explain the will. I have no idea what it says. Did Simon make one recently?'

'Yes Antoinette, after our wedding in July. He showed it to me but I did not want to know and did not understand it. There is also a matter of my naturalisation. So tomorrow. À bientôt.'

'Formidable!' Nicole said as I put my phone away.

'Quoi?'

'Tu Trudi. Formidable. I would not like to be on the wrong side of you.'

'I don't think you could be on the wrong side, Nicole. You and Sophie are my sisters, I feel so close to you.'

The food came and we ate well. I drank more and watched the people and listened to the singer. I wanted to stay there, where there was little of Simon unlike the villa which was all him. The drink did not deaden the pain. I did not get drunk, but I was slightly unsteady as a waiter held the door open for us as we left. Nicole took my arm and guided me to her car. She delivered us home safely and saw me to my bedroom.

'Would you like me to sleep with you tonight Trudi?'

I looked at her small serious face with my sight blurred by alcohol.

'Oui Nicole, merci.'

She helped me undress, putting my clothes away as I wiped the makeup from my face. I took a sleeping pill and fell asleep almost immediately.

Chapter 2.

Nicole roused me from my drug-induced sleep at six-thirty. I left my bed feeling slightly light headed, the effects of the sleeping pill still washing round my bloodstream. The pill also had deadened the absolute desolation I had felt the night before.

After showering, I dressed. I chose a bodycon dress, figure hugging, one I had picked up in a multiple, in deep dark red. I wore it with a black necklace and bracelet made of spinel, and a black patent belt, shoes and bag. I made sure that my hair was again classic, smooth princess like. My makeup was subtle, accentuating my best features. I managed a cup of coffee and a small portion of cornflakes.

Nicole was ready and waiting. I decided we would take my car and she was only too pleased to drive the Mercedes sports tourer. Expertly she drove me to the avocat (solicitors) and we arrived before the main rush hour had choked the Parisian streets.

We took the lift to the top floor and were shown into a small and comfortable conference room. The secretary offered us coffee and we both accepted. Antoinette and another woman and a young man of about thirty entered. After the introductions, Antoinette spoke first.

'Trudi, I have looked at suing the police. It is by no means certain that we could take the case to court, let alone win. It depends how strongly you feel about it. If you want to give them a nasty fright, then of course I can do that. I understand how you feel.'

'I feel strongly that Barre ignored my pleas and advice. It was absurd of him to think he had to keep Simon in a cell overnight. He was not a common criminal, but a highly respected man of means. Barre was high handed. I think he deserves a good scare at least. Can you please serve him with a writ or whatever you do, and we will see what happens. I am prepared to spend some money on revenge. Yes it is not a good emotion, but to me, it is as if Barre had killed Simon himself, by being so officious. Perhaps we need the opinion of a jurist? I leave it to you Antoinette, but I am very angry with that man.'

'We will see what can be done,' Antoinette said.

The young man spoke next. Paul Morel was a handsome fellow, very French in a dark and slightly chiselled way, almost Mediterranean. He was impeccably dressed in a dark blue suit and pink striped shirt.

'I have the will here Trudi. May I discuss it now?' He meant in the presence of Nicole.

'Nicole is my right hand Paul and also PR Marketing Director of Maison Beauvonne. Yes, I have just appointed her, she is as surprised as you, but I need a reliable person to be my councillor. Do please carry on.'

'There are three children and therefore three quarters of the estate is reserved for them. The other quarter, regardless of your nationality is reserved for you. However, you will now become managing director of the estate and

Maison Beauvonne, for which you will receive a salary, so you will be very wealthy Madame Trudi. The children inherit the estate and the business as it stands today, so we will need a valuation. However, the future profits made under your management are yours to do with as you think fit. Therefore you need not worry about money.

'As regards the children, you are not a blood relative nor do you have French nationality yet. I believe you have put in an application? Oui, quite so, and that ought to be confirmed in the next two months. Once that is a fact, there can be no challenge to your acting as the parent of the children and it was of course your husband's wish that you would do so. There is just a slight danger, that someone could challenge that until French nationality is confirmed. However, they would have to prove that you are a poor parent and unfit and that the children would benefit more by being in their care. It is most unlikely that could be proved.'

'I can confirm that Madame Trudi is an excellent mother considering her other onerous duties.' Nicole interjected.

'Good, I had no doubt it was so. Nevertheless, I propose that until your French nationality is confirmed, I act for the children, delegating care to you, and we keep the will under wraps as you say in England. Does that meet with your approval?'

'I am in your hands entirely. The French inheritance law is a mystery to me, and very unlike English law as I understand it.'

'Well it was very different, dating from Emperor Napoleon but it has been converging with English law, with the influence of European Law. We are all governed by the European Convention on Human Rights. I do not think you have to worry about it. I will just delay things until your nationality is confirmed. You are keeping British nationality too?' I nodded. 'That is your legal right and it makes no difference to this matter.

'As far as the funeral is concerned, Simon made only one request, that he be buried in the Beauvonne cemetery, next to his brother, father and mother. He has asked, which is slightly unusual, that when your time comes, you are buried next to him. He requests therefore that a space is left for that to happen, but it is by no means binding on you. You are exceedingly young, and one could reasonably expect you to remarry. However, if you do, your new spouse is prevented by covenant from inheriting any part of the estate, and that also applies to any other stepchildren you might acquire in the future, if you should remarry. I hope this puts your mind at rest?'

'Thank you. I know where I am at least. One thing bothers me still. When the children become of age, does that mean that the estate will be split up between them?'

'They will be entitled to their inheritance under the law and the terms of the will, but not until the youngest is twenty-five.'

'But that could be disastrous and ruin the estate.'

'I would recommend that you put money aside, so that they can take their share in money and the estate remains whole. That would allow André to inherit the estate and continue the line, and his brother and sister would have money to invest. This firm, will remain as managers of their rights, and you will need to make a report each year showing that the children's interests are secure. Meanwhile, and Simon said this in the will, he has every confidence that you will manage the estate, the whole of it and remain as the children's guardian. He also stated a wish that you will manage Maison Beauvonne and, I fail to see how, finish your studies.' He frowned.

'Do you have any questions?'

'No, Paul, I think you have told me all I need to know at the moment. I will keep in touch. It is satisfactory. We just need to make plenty of money and invest it wisely. If that is all, then I will leave you. I have to go to Lisieux to arrange the funeral and make sure the burial ground is reserved. Thank you so much.'

It was only just after nine and we were in the car nosing our way west towards La Défense. By ten we were in the country. I fell asleep again, curled up under the safety belt, my head against the seat back.

Nicole awakened me as we neared Lisieux. I asked her to find a hotel where I could freshen up and use the ladies. Coffee always makes me need the loo. I freshened up, but I could not remove the darkness below my eyes. I looked old. I felt old and from a life of sunshine, in two days I had moved to dullness and oppression. Where I had hope, I now saw only bleakness. Nicole stood watching me as I attended to my face.

'May I say something Trudi?'

'Of course Nicole.'

'Drop the vendetta against Barre. That is not you Trudi. You are generous and sweet, not vindictive. You have to let it go, or it will eat you.'

'He killed Simon by being so officious. I cannot forgive. I don't know what I am going to do without him.'

'Nothing will be gained by hurting Barre. Yes he was wrong, but nothing can bring Simon back.'

'Enough Nicole. I did not promote you so that you can be my conscience. Take me to the Basilique.'

'Oh so you meant that? I am now PR and marketing director?'

'Yes Nicole, of course I meant it. I trust you above everyone, even Sabine and Wally.'

'Then you must expect me to always be honest with you?'

'What sort of serpentine logic are you employing now? Yes, you have to be honest with me always.'

'Then it is my honest opinion that you should not get into a war with Barre. I say no more.'

I did not reply. We pulled up at the Basilique and entered the place where I had been so happily married just seven months ago. I found breathing difficult as we climbed the steps to the door. So many memories passed across my mind of that gorgeous day.

I am not the least religious, my logical mind cannot cope with all the canonicals and formalised prayers, nor take the bible seriously as an accurate history of anything. Even so, as we pushed through the door, I felt faint and overcome by emotion. I wanted to kneel and ask for God to wave his magic wand and bring Simon back. In my disturbed state, I almost believed it could happen. Nicole took my hand and I squeezed hers as reassurance that I appreciated her honesty and support.

Nicole spoke to an official and we were conducted to an office. I recognised the Bishop of Bayeux with two other priests. He rose as I entered.

'Come and sit my child,' he said, offering me a chair.

'Now, how may we help you?'

'It is the funeral of my husband, Simon de Beauvonne. I would like to have it here, where we can receive so many mourners. Then he will be buried in Beauvonne in the family grave. I am hoping that you are able to do this next week.'

'Of course Madame Chartrand. What days are free,' he asked one of the priests.

'Wednesday is entirely free Évêque.'

'Is that suitable Madame? Can you make arrangements in time?'

'I don't know. Perhaps Friday, is that possible?'

'Not in the afternoon. It would have to be at 10.30 Madame.'

'Then so be it. Friday at 10.30. Can we discuss the service now?'

'If you know what you require? The service will last nearly an hour according to the content. You have to decide what music you require, whether on the organ or the orchestra. We use the same musicians as at your wedding Madame, but you must decide on the music soon because they and the choir need to practice. We have a list of their repertoire but you must let us know tomorrow which music you want.'

A priest gathered papers together and handed them to me in a card wallet, blue with a gold cross upon the front.

'Read through the information and phone us tomorrow with your decisions.'

'Thank you Évêque. I will. I have much to do now, if you will pardon me. À bientôt.'

We shook hands, the Bishop holding my hand and sandwiching it with his other. It was somehow embarrassing. I did not know whether I was expected to curtsy or kiss his hand. I was glad to be outside, even on this grey cold January day.

'Beauvonne Nicole please. I think we need to eat too. Rive Droite I think Nicole. We have had happy times there.'

As usual, we were well received and had a good light lunch of seafood salad. It was delightful but I had to force myself to eat.

'Nicole, you are right. Hurting Barre will do no good. It will just carry on the hurt.' Somehow the atmosphere of that great Basilique had calmed me, even though we had not lingered or prayed. 'I will phone Antoinette. Thank you Nicole. You are a true friend. It was a good day when you appeared in Moutier and we met. We have much to do. We must try and get the caterers we used for the wedding. Can you do that this afternoon? If they can do it, then we cater for five hundred, the same names and addresses of the wedding guests. Not all will come. Then phone Clermont Ferrand. They can arrange coaches. The Basilique at 10.30 then Lunch here at one o'clock. And phone Thomas and Jacques. They can arrange the Paris coaches. Can you do all this, this afternoon? I will email family and friends myself, and work on the ceremony. Oh, the catering. Use your judgement as to the menu. Two starters, three main dishes something like a meat and a fish and a vegetarian dish, and a sweet, I think an apple pie Normande and ice-cream. I will see if I can find who supplied the wine for the wedding. Let's get to Beauvonne and start work.'

We worked well into the evening with just bread and cheese and coffee as refreshment. Sabine assisted us, taking care of all the French side of the family, once again using Simon's records of the wedding.

My brother agreed to bring mother and father, but most of my friends and relatives could not come. At least they were all informed of my loss. Nicole sat back and yawned. 'Have we done everything Trudi?'

'I hope so Nicole, except we have to speak to the local priest about the burial. Oh and I promised to phone the undertaker about the coffin and burial day. First thing tomorrow.' I wrote a post it note. 'And the Mairie, I hope that is all.' I wrote another post it note. 'Bedtime. Wake me at nine if I am still asleep would you please? Thank you both for your help. I don't know what I would have done without you.'

I looked forward to taking another sleeping pill to rest my tired mind.

Chapter 3.

The next week went by in a blur. Nicole shepherded me about, keeping me on course. I drank rather more than I should, trying to dull the awful pain within, the vast emptiness I felt at the loss of Simon. It seemed like a vacuum within my breast, sucking the life out of me.

Somehow I survived the funeral. It was a truly grand affair, attended by even more people than our wedding of just months ago. Even as I thought of the short time since that glorious 15th July day when life had become so sweet, my stomach twisted and turned inside me. I wanted to curl up into a ball, woodlice like, hide my tortured face away and show just a hard carapace to the World. I could not. Instead I deadened the pain with my sleeping pills and alcohol.

My family made the journey, did their best to comfort me, my brother especially tender, then they were gone, the last of the mourners to depart.

I rode Sheba, I tended the children and slopped about the estate in clothes that once I would not have been seen dead in. I leant on Nicole more and more.

Paul Morel was a frequent visitor. I looked forward to his coming, not because he was attractive sexually, which he was, but it was good to have someone looking after all the legal matters that I hardly understood. French inheritance law seemed very involved and I was glad to have a lawyer who was also a friend looking after matters for me.

I had passed from being a strong and vibrant personality, a woman bursting with ideas and energy when Simon was alive, to being an automaton. Nicole, a month after the funeral took me to task.

'Trudi, I am sorry to see you so distraught, but you have to snap out of it. Things need your attention. We, Sophie, Sabine, Wally and I are doing our best to hold things together, but affairs need you. You should not be like this now.'

'I am grieving Nicole. Simon was my husband but also my creator. You don't know……, how much it hurts.'

'We'll give you a bit longer, but you have to get a grip. And you are drinking too much.'

I made no reply. I had made Nicole, now she was lecturing me. I did not say, but I thought, what right has she to speak so? I could not be bothered to reply. Even a sunny day seemed grey and foggy.

Spring came and I hardly noticed when once I would have been joyful at every new green shoot I observed. The lambs were born and I hardly noticed them either.

Bathing Sébastien, I fell asleep. Sophie was shocked, and thereafter I was not trusted to be alone with the children.

Paul came with papers to sign. It was nice to see him, to speak to an intelligent young man. He told me that he had seats to a concert.

'If you are in Paris, it would be good for you to see something different. Would you come?'

'What is it?'

'Beethoven's Ninth and Mozart's piano concerto 21 the beautiful Elvira Madigan. Very emotional.'

'They would make me cry. I would not be good company.'

'Perhaps you need to cry instead of being the iron maiden. It is a box, so take a box of tissues. No one will see you cry. I shall not mind if you break down. Wear a black veil to hide your face, that should appeal to your dramatic instincts.'

In my befuddled self-pity, I did not understand the sleight.

'Perhaps.'

'No not perhaps. You must decide now. Say you will come.'

'Well, they tell me that there are affairs to be decided at the Maison, so very well Paul. Thank you. I do not mean to be off hand, it is just that I miss Simon so.'

'I know you do. The concert is next Wednesday. I look forward to seeing you then. I do understand your grief, but it will do you good to get out into society. No one doubts the love you had for each other. I will come to the villa for you, then we will have dinner after the concert. After all, with the legal fees you are paying, I should be able to treat my client.'

When he had gone, I told Nicole about it.

'Good. It is a start Trudi. We all miss our vivacious princess. We will drive to Paris on Monday and spend all day in the Maison. We have designs to look at and a show to put together. You know I too need help. We have lost three senior staff, Gérard and Annette and especially Simon. You can't leave it all to Wally and me.'

'I am sorry Nicole, you must think me self-indulgent. I will make an effort.'

'Trudi, I love you and love the job. Grief takes people in different ways, but you, I expected more, because you are so strong. You have always gone for it, whatever life has thrown at you. I know some of your history from Wally. He cannot understand this behaviour either. I am here for you, but I cannot carry you.'

I started to pull myself together. I stopped drinking so much and cut the sleeping pill to half enough at least to get me to sleep. I started to run each day as soon as I awoke, running for half an hour then back to shower and dress, becoming the princess again, outwardly at least. Inside my heart still screamed, my Simon, my Simon. If I spoke his name, tears formed and speech became impossible.

The only other man I saw in this time was Wally. I was aware that all my friends had been patronising me, protecting me, whispering about me, but I could not be bothered. Gradually I found pride again.

Nicole, the designers and I sorted out things at the Maison. We arranged a meeting of all the department heads and directors for the following week. I felt better for being busy and needed. My friends had indulged my grief and I had fed on it, lapping at their indulgence. Looking back, I was ashamed. Work was the best medicine. Sometimes, often, pity fuels self-pity. Sometimes one needs a good friend, to give one a good kick in the pants. Nicole had been there for me.

On the Wednesday morning, Paul phoned to make sure I was still going to the concert. He seemed pleased that I answered yes.

Nicole and I shared Simon's office, both sitting at his large desk. We composed an advert for an office manager. There were other things I should do too she said, like do a tour of all the shops with Wally and go to Clermont Ferrand. I agreed. I would plan it after next week's meeting.

Paul picked me up at seven. The concert was nearby at La Madeleine. I did not consider this a date but a night out as business associates. I dressed conservatively, a grey wool dress and matching jacket with some sequin detailing on the collar.

Paul was attentive and well mannered. He was in what goes for evening dress for the young generation, fancy white shirt, evening suit but the tie untied and just hanging. Maybe he could not do the knot or maybe that was dressing down a dress suit.

We took our seats. The uplifting strains of the Beethoven started and I lost myself in the music. I had not listened to either piece with Simon, in fact, although I had heard the Mozart before, I had not known what it was. I did cry, not so much from the music, but from thinking how Simon would have loved this. He had taught me so much about culture, the real things that mattered in our European society. Freedom of expression, acceptance of ideas, art in all its forms, music and literature, science and invention. Yes there were over indulgent things like haute couture, nouveau cuisine, the outrageous concoctions from some Michelin star kitchens, but it was all taking human artistry to the last possible degree.

I realised as I sat listening to Elvira Madigan, that my view of the World from France was considerably different from the one I would have possessed in England. Here in this very nationalist nation, the French were French to the core, but also believed in Europe and its culture and valued it above all. From here, the UK looked barbarous in comparison, insular, not because its arts were indifferent, they certainly were not, but because culture seemed to permeate deeper into French society without so much North American influence.

Memories of my past life flashed through my mind. For the last nine years, Simon had been my God, steering me though my difficult life, showing me this golden culture of the European, dressing me, protecting me, introducing me to Parisian society. Now he was gone and I had to stand on my own feet, make all my own decisions. I had responsibilities and I knew that I could take them on. Maison Beauvonne, Chateau Beauvonne, the children and all my family, Nicole, Sophie, Sabine and Wally, all the staff. They all depended on me. I had to find the energy to take things forward. Simon was my beautiful past, but I had to look to the future.

By the time we left the concert, I was dry eyed. Paul took my arm as we found our way through the crowds and crossed the street. We continued to walk up Rue Faubourg St Honoré, his arm in mine and I found it comforting. We entered the Hotel Bristol and I was surprised to find that we were going into the Restaurant L'Epicure with three Michelin stars. I wished I had dressed for it.

'This costs a small fortune Paul. Are you sure? Let us each pay for what we have at least.'

'Do you wish to insult me, Madame Chartrand?'

'Of course not, but I have money. Why should I take yours?'

'Oh don't worry, I am sure you will pay for it in my fees.'

I smiled. We had beautiful food, tiny portions of exquisitely designed dishes, each one a picture. I finished with a net ball of chocolate which contained what looked at first like a golden mouse within. I could not work out how they could make such an object. We had drunk champagne throughout the meal. Paul wanted to take a taxi, but I asked to walk. The night was fine and warm for April and I wished to clear my head. He took my hand as we made our way to the villa and I did not protest.

He said there were some papers to sign and I took them to the hall table, signing obediently where he indicated. We said goodbye at the door of the villa Paul kissed me on both cheeks and then surprisingly on the lips. I ignored it. I quite liked it though, and it was flattering. He was handsome, clean, manly and pleasant company. He was no Simon, but he had treated me well enough.

'We must do this again. Perhaps not so luxuriously Trudi, but it would do us both good to see more of what this marvellous city has to offer, n'est- ce pas?'

'Oui Paul, but I am not ready for a romance. It is too early.'

'Of course Trudi. I hope I have not been too forward. It has been a pleasure. I will phone you.'

I had warned him off. I liked him but I did not like him enough, even as a tool to overcome my grief and loss. He phoned next day and we made a date to go to the theatre next week.

Nicole continued with our work. She was right, there was much to do. We drew up an agenda for the meeting next week, and emailed it to everyone, asking them to reply with a report on their current activities and aims.

Nicole moved to her old office and I interviewed each and every one of the Paris staff, finding out about them, their families, ambitions and their jobs. By the end of the week I felt more confident of running this great enterprise. The staff were largely happy, just to be employed was a good thing in these days of depression, but to be valued and asked for ideas and ambitions was a bonus to them. There were one or too who needed to sharpen up, but mostly they were a good bunch. I gave the less enthusiastic a chance to come back to me with ideas for their future, jobs in the organisation that they thought would be more appropriate and promised to see what could be done, hoping to motivate them. I was polite to them, but I let them know that others were more ambitious and potentially valuable to Beauvonne. At the end of the week I brought everyone together in the Salon and made a little speech, asking for support and ideas so that we could all enjoy a profitable future.

Afterwards Nicole offered her congratulations. 'Merci ma Princesse. It is good to have the real Trudi back.'

'And thank you Nicole. I shall not forget what I owe you. It was a good day when Sophie suggested you as my assistant. We will go far together I am sure.'

The meeting the week after was educational and enjoyable. On the whole I found Beauvonne in a good state of health. Clermont Ferrand still had capacity to make more and there was a difficulty in making short runs of items. We would either have to cut some lines from production or find new ways of marketing them. It needed a deal of thought and I put the problem firmly in Wally's court. There were certain other matters that needed attention, but on the whole, the organisation was highly motivated and enthusiastic. They were anxious to prove something to me, the new directrice.

Paul took me to a few more concerts. He never kissed me on the lips again. In truth, he was a diversion but I soon tired of his company. He was actually quite boring, with a limited experience of life, and quite disinterested in my life. I began to dread his phone calls and made excuses. Our meetings grew less and less. I signed more papers concerning nationality and the children's inheritance at his direction, then our outings ceased. With the business in good order, I arranged visits to our various outlets with Wally. We started with the new store in Dubai, from there we flew to Hong Kong and on to Shanghai. I was impressed with Wally's command of the stores and personnel. He made excellent suggestions regarding stock they should hold and negotiated prices with them on stock that was hanging.

We were well received everywhere until we reached LA. They seemed out of sorts with us, saying that our penetration of the celebrity market there was being eroded by other houses who were more free with loan dresses for the never ending events for the A listers. I promised a more relaxed attitude to these over paid bloodsuckers. One had to think about the larger picture. A star in a Beauvonne dress at the Emmys or Oscars was worth more than a dress on the catwalk in Paris or New York. Women were avid readers of the reports on those occasions, especially the photos in Vogue or OK and the rest.

We moved on to New York and planned our biggest show ever there for the autumn. We returned to Paris and I was glad to be home.

I was disturbed that I had still not heard from Paul regarding my guardianship of the children and of my nationality. I phoned Paul's office twice and found he was not there. In desperation I phoned Antoinette.

'How can we help you Trudi.'

'I haven't heard from Paul Morel, and he hasn't answered my calls. I am worried about my affairs.'

'He has left us Trudi, I am afraid under a bit of a cloud.'

'Oh why? I thought he was so able.'

'We did not approve of his methods, so he was asked to resign. Personally I think he should have been dismissed. I think you need to look into your affairs in case you have received the same treatment. I know that you have met him on several social occasions. We were on the point of writing to you about one or two matters concerning the conduct of your affairs, but some things have fallen beyond our control.'

'Now I am worried. Can I come in and see you, and his successor.'

'Of course. Let me make some arrangements and I will get back to you with a time. In the meantime sign no more papers.'

I was very frightened. Had all the contacts with Paul, the meal at Epicure, the concerts and plays and the kiss on the lips been an act, grooming me for the kill. I hoped not. I had signed so many papers of which I knew nothing. What a fool I had been. I would never trust another soul.

I called Nicole in. We now had the last few applicants for office manager to see, and we cut the short list to make our task easier, hoping that we had not eliminated a really good prospect because their experience was lacking.

Antoinette phoned with an appointment in two days time, the first date they could get all the members of the firm together.

I started on the interviews with Nicole's help. Eventually we settled on a middle-aged woman who had worked for Naf Naf as a buyer but was also trained in human resources. She seemed perfect.

On my desk the next day, I found a letter with printed on the outside Paul Morel, Avocat.

The letter informed me that I should vacate Chateau Beauvonne. As the children's guardian, he was lawfully taking possession of the Chateau on behalf of the children and a court had decided that I was a bad influence on the children to whom I was not related. I was to be allowed the Paris villa as Managing Director of Maison Beauvonne, over which he had no jurisdiction. My fears were confirmed. In my indulgent grief, I had been a trusting fool. Simon's carefully laid plans, the death of Catherine, our marriage, and all the time I had spent with the children, counted for nothing and were negated by a grasping lawyer. Well, he would find that I would fight and I was determined to win.

The days before my meeting with Antoinette and the lawyers, seemed to pass very slowly. As usual I took Nicole with me for the meeting.

Lawyers all seem very civilised people, sometimes too civilised because the law does not always follow what is right and what is wrong. Oh yes they follow the law but sometimes that is far removed from natural justice. In this instance I was in the right, but according to them, Paul Morel was in the right because he had obtained my signature. That he had acquired that signature by subterfuge, seemed not to matter. In my grief and confusion after Simon's death, I had signed away the children and the Beauvonne estate.

We sat round a highly polished table in a featureless room, Antoinette, the new family lawyer, Boris Sanson and a fraud lawyer, Serge Divanchy. They were absolved of all wrongdoing and it was apparently my own fault. I asked whether I should sue their firm, as Paul had set out to defraud me. They did not like that. They would see what could be done, but intimated that it might take years and millions of Euros fighting it through the courts.

After an hour, we had got nowhere. I thanked them for their time and we departed. How a firm could absolve itself of the wrong doing of its employee, I just did not understand. I had been a client of the firm not Paul Morel who merely represented the firm.

As Nicole and I walked back to the office I said, 'Nicole, I think I am going to find a less legal way of regaining the children and the Chateau.'

'Then you must be careful Trudi. I know nothing, but how will you do it?'

'I don't know yet, but I will find a way. We have to make Paul hand over those papers and renounce his guardianship first. After that, I do not care what happens to Paul Morel. Tonight, I think we will have a cheap Italian meal at Franco's Nicole, unless you have other plans?'

'No other plans Trudi. Thomas is away looking at fabrics, so Italian will do fine.'

Franco was his usual over the top self, welcoming me with kisses, hanging on to my hand and treating Nicole in the same way. We both chose his dish of the day, lasagne al forno.

It was a slow night, only two other tables occupied. Franco came to sit with us after we had finished our sweet and were drinking coffee.

'I am so sorry to see that Monsieur Simon had died. My condolences Madame. How are you?'

'I have been ill Franco, not medically ill, but in grief. I could not do anything. Nicole, my good friend, has looked after me, but now I am strong again.'

'So things are better now. It always takes time, especially when you have such deep love.'

'Franco you have always been a good friend. While I was so frail, I made a bad mistake. I trusted a lawyer and he has taken advantage of my trust. Nicole, perhaps you would like to get a taxi home while I discuss a matter with Franco?'

'Madame, let Nicole wait for you in my small salon.'

Nicole looked at me quizzically. I nodded and Franco escorted her to the back. When he returned I said, 'Franco, it is not that I do not trust Nicole, I just do not want her involved. Some time ago, someone told me that you are a person one can trust, that you have connections. Is that true?'

'I know what they say, that I am Mafiosi. I know people. Me, mafia, oh no, a fat old man like me? But I know people of influence of course. They are useful friends. Do you have much trouble Madame?'

I told him of Paul Morel and how in my despair he had dispossessed me. 'So you see Franco, I need advice. I want the Chateau and above all, I want the children. The Chateau is their inheritance, and Paul Morel has no right to any part of it, nor any right to go against the will of Simon who wanted me to look after his children, our children, for I feel they are rightfully mine.'

'It is a big problem Madame, not an easy one to resolve. Let me think about it. I will find a solution, never fear. I know a lawyer, a good customer and friend, who is the most discreet person. I phone you when I know what to do. Tell no one, but I see you are discreet too, even with your friend. It is tricky, but there will be a way.'

He produced liqueurs and we joined Nicole who was talking to Madame Franco. We stayed another hour. Franco called a taxi to take us home.

'What did you talk to Franco about Trudi?'

'Private business Nicole. I do not want you involved.'

'You can trust me, and I want to help.'

'Of course I trust you, but for your own safety Nicole, in case something goes wrong, I am not involving you in this.'

'Then I do not ask, but I am here for you Trudi.'

'I know you are Nicole, but it is best you know nothing.'

Chapter 4.

I spent the next week in the Maison with Mademoiselle Devreau, the office manager. She seemed very competent and was soon working with the designers and the cutting room. She sorted out the pay, tut-tutting over the books left by Gérard.

Nicole and I went to Vesuvio everyday for lunch, a light snack and coffee. 'Nicole, I think we should appoint an accountant, to keep an eye on our expenditure and as a check on Martine Devreau. Do you know of anyone?'

'No Trudi, but perhaps if we put a notice in the office one of the staff will know someone. It will be like keeping it in the family.'

'We can try that first. I'll do that this afternoon.' I was interrupted my phone bouncing on the table.

Franco said just one sentence. 'I have your account Madame, perhaps you will call?' The phone went dead.

'I have something to attend to Nicole. Will you pay the bill and this afternoon, put that advertisement on the board and make sure all the staff see it.'

I walked to Franco's. The bell tinkled gaily as I pushed the frosted glass door open. Madame Franco came to welcome me and led me through the deserted tables to the back parlour.

'My husband has just gone to the wholesaler, he will be back in a few minutes. Would you like a glass of wine Madame Trudi?'

"Non merci Madame. Du café s'il vous plait?'

'Mais oui.' She produced coffee and we chatted about her brood of children as they entered from school.

Franco appeared after what seemed a long time. We got down to business with the help of a glass of liqueur.

'Firstly, you have to get the court ruling changed. There are two ways, well maybe four of changing a man's mind. Money, sex, blackmail or torture. By what you tell me, this man dated you then discarded you, so I do not think sex will work. We could try blackmail, but we would need to frame him. I would like to use torture, but I do not think so. We have to tempt him with money. We will send him a messenger, a solicitor of our acquaintance. He will offer Morel a million Euros, 250,000 now and the balance when the legalities are in order. We need you to supply the 250,000 Euros and that will be our fee for doing this. That is all you have to do. Is it agreeable?'

'This will work?'

'Oh we do not expect a refusal. We may have to offer more than a million but that does not matter. He will not receive it. So how soon can you get the money?'

'In a few days. I don't know, I have never tried to get that much money before.'

'But you can supply us with 250,000?'

'Oh yes Franco. I have the money.'

'The sooner you get the money, the sooner you are reunited with the children and the Chateau. It is up to you Madame Trudi. But a word of warning, try to get the money from different sources, so that the exact amount is not seen as passing from you to him. Have you something you can sell or pawn?'

'I can sell Simon's Mercedes saloon and sports. I don't really like them and it would seem natural after his death to sell them. I have my Convertible, which was a present from Simon. Then I have a diamond choker. I could porn that. The rest I can get from the bank, but it will all take a few days.'

'I suggest then that you set things in motion. Our lawyer will contact Morel and present the deal and see what he says. It should be an offer that is impossible to turn down.'

'Thank you Franco. I will let you know as soon as I have the money.'

'Perhaps you will contact Morel and ask to see him? Find out where he is living. Not at the Chateau I presume?'

'I believe he has had a couple of weekends there, with friends shooting, but that is all.'

'Then he has a flat in Paris. It would be good if he lives alone, but it is not essential.'

'I will phone this afternoon.'

'Good. Morel will soon be out of your life Madame if you do as we ask.'

I phoned before I reached home.

'Paul. It is Trudi. I wonder whether we could meet. No I would rather not at your office. You have a house or apartment in Paris?'

He gave an address on Rue Dauphine, on the left bank opposite Notre Dame. I was surprised that he agreed to meet me at his flat, but then he had the upper hand, and we had been out together several times, even though his motive had been one of personal gain. I would find it hard to be civil, but I must be if he was to take the bait and agree to be bought out of his interest in Beauvonne.

For an hour after I put the phone down I could think of nothing else than my meeting. I put poor neglected Tasha's lead on and we made for the Seine. I walked her through the Tuileries. We crossed the road and down the steps to the embankment and turned down river towards Pont de l'Alma. We sat on a bench and considered the grey waters.

I was taking a great risk involving Franco, but the stakes were high. I had now been away from the children for two months. Sophie phoned with reports of them and Nicole had been to see them and her sister Sophie of course. Paul had visited just twice, but paid them no attention. His guardianship was therefore just a fraud, yet legally he held all the cards. I suspected that we were going to offer exactly what he wanted.

I would play the distraught stepmother tomorrow, and see what happened. Perhaps he would soften and save me some money. If he did not then I would let Franco's plan proceed. Whatever happened then, would be due to his response.

On the way home I called at the shops and bought fish and meat, some new potatoes and fennel and baby spinach. We returned to the villa and I cooked for Nicole and Martin who was coming home with her and also for Élise and Jean Luc. I looked forward to hearing all their news from the hospital. I brought up two bottles of champagne and set the table, using my best cutlery and glasses.

I took trouble over my dress, a knee length dark blue silk number, simple in form but with self-coloured embroidery. It had been the last dress Simon had brought home for me. I did my hair and makeup carefully.

Nicole and Martin arrived just before six and Élise and Jean Luc, just after seven thirty. We had aperitifs in the salon, and while they all chatted, I finished off the cooking.

We started with sole bonne femme and moved on to filet steaks. As we ate, Jean Luc said, 'Is this a special occasion Trudi.'

Before I could answer, Nicole spoke, 'Oui, ma Princesse est de retour.'

Martin stood, 'It is good. I would like to make a toast. Here is to Trudi, Comtesse de Beauvonne. We are glad to have her back in the family from her dark place.'

'Thank you Martin. It is good to be back. Especially, my thanks to Nicole for being the best of friends, one who always speaks the truth, even when it hurts. Beauvonne is going to do great things I am sure. You are my family, and I love you all. Thank you for not giving up on me.'

Next day I worked with the designers in the morning, reviewing the designs for the summer show. I ate lunch with Nicole and Martine Devreau. I was then going home to get ready to see Paul. I asked Nicole if she would allow me to borrow her phone and she handed it over without question. The day was cool and had clouded over.

At the villa I changed into my grey wool dress and put on a light loose fitting raincoat. I placed my fully charged phone in a pocket and Nicole's phone switched off in my bag.

I arrived at Morel's flat at four thirty-four, just four minutes late. Paul answered the door almost immediately.

'Come in Trudi. I don't know what you want but I can offer you a glass of wine or coffee at least.'

'Perhaps a coffee then Paul.'

He disappeared into the kitchen. I could see him moving about through the opened doorway. I looked around the room. It was minimalist and quite masculine. A black leather suite, a large bookcase full of mostly law books and novels, a forty inch plus TV slapped on the wall and a coffee table. There was one picture on the wall, which had at one time resided in Simon's study, a little known late impressionist, Leo Vilhar. It was not worth much, but I liked it and it was part of Simon who had treasured it above its value. I took Nicole's phone from my bag switched it on and placed it on the table so he could see it.

Paul brought in the coffee in a filter jug and clinked cups and saucers onto the table.

'So what can I do for you Trudi Chartrand?'

'I asked to see you here rather than make a public scene.'

'So have you come to plead with me Trudi, for the estate and the children?'

'I cannot understand why I have been deprived of them. Why did you do that? I thought you were my friend.'

He picked up Nicole's phone and checked it. He switched it off, waiting until the screen had gone blank.

'I needed to get to know you so I could set up on my own. We were never friends. It was business. You were in a state too, mooning about over your bereavement. I found it a bit pathetic.'

'But to take away the children, against Simon's wishes and to have me banished from the Chateau. What harm had I done?'

'None. It was business. I needed capital. I still need capital. I do not intend to live in this small flat forever. You had all the trappings of the rich, jewellery, smart cars, the ski chalet, which incidentally is still in your name and Maison Beauvonne. And who are you? You are good-looking, yes beautiful, but you are not a woman Trudi. I don't get this transsexual thing. I mean, God, it's disgusting and to think

Simon Chartrand, Comte de Beauvonne actually married you, and at Lisieux.'

'How cruel you are Paul. We went out together on several occasions. You held my hand and, yes even kissed me on the lips. And that is how you felt?'

'I was nearly sick, but it was worth it.'

'So it was all an act.' I allowed a sob and a tear involuntarily appeared, caused by his cruelty and the doubts about myself, that I could not shake off.

I took a sip of coffee and dabbed my eye.

'I would like that picture Paul. It was one of Simon's favourites. It is worth at the very most, €10,000. I will give you a cheque for €15,000, now, please, it means so much.

He studied me for a minute. He smiled. 'If it means that much. Write the cheque.'

I wrote the cheque. He perused it and laid it on the table. 'So what did you really want to see me about?'

'I want the children back. My French nationality is now confirmed. Antoinette sorted that out. And I want the Chateau back.'

'You will understand that leaving the firm to go on my own has been an expense, and then getting a court order against you, although not difficult given your past and knowing the right magistrate, has also cost. I still need more money, quite a lot of money, particularly to wipe the taste of your mouth from my lips.' He let that insult sink in. He smirked. 'So make me an offer.'

'I can't now. I thought you would just be reasonable, as a friend. I did not expect this.'

'I should have gone on the stage, my act must have been convincing. Surely, you did not come here thinking I would just give it all back. For nothing? So what are you going to do?'

'I will check my finances. I can probably find a hundred thousand for you to reverse whatever you have done.'

'It will have to be more than that. Considerably more, and I know you have it.'

'You do not know the state of Maison Beauvonne. We have had great expense with machinery in Clermont Ferrand, and sales of the latest collection were not good in this depression. I will take advice, see what I can sell, and I will send someone to negotiate. You will understand Paul, that I do not wish to see you again, knowing how you feel about me.'

'That will be fine, but don't take too long.'

'By the end of the week Paul. You will have an offer. I will send a trusted friend to negotiate. By the way, I despise you too.'

'It is business Trudi, that's all.'

I left the coffee mostly untouched. I walked up Rue Dauphine towards the Pont Neuf carrying the unwrapped picture. I would have to go to the Chateau and make sure he had not sold the whole contents. Sophie had not told me of anything missing, so perhaps this picture had ben a one off.

I could not find a taxi until I reached the river, and the weight of the heavy frame was pulling the picture wire deep into my palm. I sobbed as I sat in the cab. I felt sick, disgusted, demoralised. I dabbed my eyes dry, took a grip of myself. I took my phone from my bag and checked it. It had faithfully recorded everything we had said. I phoned Nicole.

'Nicole I am on my way home. Are you free tonight?'

'I can be Trudi. What do you have in mind?'

'I have some complimentary tickets for Coldplay at Stade Francais. Would you come.'

'Of course. You are on your way home?'

'A minute or two away. I want to see Franco too.'

'Ah, cloak and dagger. Of course. À bientôt.'

Chapter 5.

In the villa, I quickly downloaded the recording I had made of my conversation with Paul. I checked the two CDs I had made and found they were fine. For good measure, I also recorded it on a USB. I locked the USB and one disc in the safe. The other I put in my bag for Franco.

I changed into jeans and a bomber jacket and we set out for Stade Francais, finding a taxi on Boulevard Haussmann. My VIP tickets got us in straight away and we found ourselves standing in front of the stage, our electric armbands around our wrists. I told Nicole of my afternoon and what Paul Morel had said. She was truly shocked.

'You are a girl to me, could not be more so, and you are my Princess. Really Trudi, I never think of you as anything else.'

'I know. Thank you, but it is my own insecurity that makes remarks like that, hurt so. I wish I could have been the boy I was supposed to be, but I could not.'

Her only answer was to hug me. Those around probably thought we were a couple of lesbians. The music began and the place started to rock. The familiar tunes and riffs beat in our ears, and we lost all fears and reason for the next ninety minutes. By the end we were glowing and on a musical high. We found ourselves shepherded towards the dressing rooms and were introduced to the band along with a lot of other celebs, some of whom I knew slightly. I looked at Nicole, and we spoke to each other without words and slipped out of the melée.

After walking for what seemed a long way, arm in arm, we found a taxi. Safely in side, Nicole started to laugh.

'What is so amusing?'

'You, wishing you could have been a boy? It is absurd. There is not the remotest chance. And remember, Simon could have married anyone, but he chose you.'

I started to laugh, and this time tears of mirth appeared. I wiped away my tears as we cruised to a stop at Franco's. On entering we found there were still people eating. Franco led us to a secluded table. We chose spaghetti carbonara and a bottle of Montepulciano 2003, which Franco assured was nectar.

It was a beautiful wine. Apparently I was now one of Franco's people, offered the best. When we finished, Franco asked if he could sit. I did not banish Nicole. I handed Franco a package containing the CD I had made and said I would speak to him later.

'It is not necessary Madame Trudi. All is taken care of.'

'First though Franco, I want to assure myself that all is well at the Chateau. He had already stolen one painting, which he sold back to me. I must make sure that he has stolen nothing else.'

'You can do this soon? And you have the fee for the solicitor who will negotiate?'

'Everything is in order. The fee is in the package.'

'Good. Then perhaps you can phone me tomorrow Madame to say we can negotiate?'

'Bien sûr Franco. Till tomorrow.'

On the way home I asked Nicole to be available for me in the morning. We would both go to Beauvonne. She would have to go in and check the rooms as I was still banned until Paul had removed the legal objections. I did not want any infringements of Paul's legal tangle to muddle my claim. I told Nicole to look for light patches on the walls, denoting where pictures could have been and to make sure the furniture was genuine. I could also not upset the children by appearing and disappearing.

I would ring Sabine and meet her on the estate away from the Chateau, while Nicole checked the rooms.

In spite of Paul's harshness, I slept well. I would soon be shot of him I hoped, and I would have the beloved children back.

I drove to Beauvonne, the first long journey as driver since the death of Simon. I had shaken off the insults of yesterday. After all, Paul was just one man, an ambitious, over eagerly ambitious nobody. Why should one man's opinion offend me? One can't expect every person in this world to like one or respect ones course in this mire we call life. However, those who deliberately set out to damage or inflict pain, should pay a price and according to Franco, Paul Morel would be broken. I had to decide this day, whether I could live with that.

They say revenge is sweet, but it is a bitter sweetness which can fester into regret. I hoped that the course I was on now, with Franco at the helm, would not give me shame in the future. It would depend on how matters went when the negotiator met Paul.

I dropped Nicole at the gates to the Chateau and watched as she walked the avenue. I drove round to the west side of the estate to a point not far from where I had been thrown from Sheba. I found Sabine waiting, sat in her Land Rover.

'Sabine,' we embraced like lovers. At length, she held me off, looking into my face.

'I can see the pain and stress you have been under my dear friend. Does this visit mean there will be a resolution to this ridiculous state of affairs?'

'Sabine, I trust you as I trust no one else, you know that. You hold secrets that you and I alone know. Paul that traitor, has made this mess for personal gain. I am checking today, to see that he has not purloined or sold the furnishings. Nicole is there now. Then tomorrow someone will meet with Morel and come to an arrangement. When he has undone this mess, he will be paid. That is all I wish you to know.'

'I know you Trudi. Evil as Morel is, you will regret dealing with him. Just remember the evil he has done, to you, to the children and all of us who have lived these four months in uncertainty.'

'Well, according to how negotiations go and what he says, his fate will be decided. He will either be penniless or, well, we will not talk about it. Now, tell me about you and Wally. Still good? Not changed your mind about this undemonstrative Englishman?'

'Oh I am learning to live with that. He is sometimes very quiet. Are all Englishmen like that? Oh yes we are on course for the wedding Trudi and you are still matron of honour, I hope?'

'It is an honour I will not miss for anything. I don't know many Englishmen. My father was often away with the fairies and it is a frequent complaint of English wives, they tell their husbands things and they do not listen. I had a different relationship with Wally. We were like brother and sister those last two years at school. He was a rufty tufty rugger player and I was learning how to be a young lady. He was so good to me then. After Simon, he is the man I would most trust.

'Oh I think in a bad situation, I would be in safe hands. He is reliable too. If he makes a promise he will keep it. It is just that he is not very romantic, even in the bedroom and I think that is my fault.'

I remained silent for a time, thinking what to say.

'I don't know what to say Sabine. I cannot advise you. I am mixed up enough myself. You are both very dear to me and I was so happy to see you together. Only you know whether you should wed, but I do know, if there are doubts, time will not heal them.' We were both silent for a time. I tried to move to a safer subject. 'And the estate, how are things? Are we making plenty of money?'

'The plan I made when I was appointed estate manager is on track. I have had to tweak a few things, but profits are actually better than I forecast. I am exceptionally proud of what I have achieved in just a year. So I am very happy. I told Morel that harvest had been poor. He looked at the books, but he is no accountant and swallowed whatever I told him. What he did not see was grain and potatoes and sugar beat in store and not yet paid for. They are all sold, but I held the cheques back until you had regained control. Nicole has kept us informed of what has been going on. I am sorry that you have had such a bad time Trudi. By what you say, things are going to get back to normal. But we have held things together here.'

'That is good to hear Sabine, thank you, but I knew you would. Let's go to that café we once went to before, when you were planning the estate. Nicole will phone when she has done.'

It was nearly two when Nicole phoned. She'd had lunch with her sister and the children. She could not find anything of note missing from the Chateau. I collected her and we headed back to Paris. I phoned Franco to go ahead.

I got down to work. I drove to Ferrand to see the factory. The production manager George Thibeau, showed me round. He would like to be busier, he said, a third of the factory was not used. I asked what he could suggest as new lines?

'We have leather workers in the town who have not worked at their trade for years. If there was leather work, bomber jackets, leather trousers, genuine motorcycle wear, we could be more productive.'

'I think we should keep with the dress trade. I would not include motorcycle wear in that, but leather goods in the fashion trade I can see. Rather than motorcycle jackets, what do you say to handbags and luggage? Have you workers in the town who could do high class work? There is a lot of money in it, enormous profits.'

George smiled. 'Yes, we certainly have, but we would need designs from someone who understands bag production.'

'So I would need to find someone in Paris. I will look into it.'

I looked over the whole factory, marvelling at the speed the workers worked on piece rate. Their production was better than production figures for China, but each worker was paid at nearly twice as much in France. There were other compensations though. Quality was better in France, reliability and turn round times, from design to the finished article being available in shops, was so much better, a tenth of the time. On quality goods therefore, European production was the best option.

I stayed the night. Next day I took the familiar road to Courchevel to see the Chalet. I had ideas to make a few changes. It was a place with so many memories of Simon and I needed to make it my own. The season was over, so the Alpine town was empty. I found a room in the best hotel and phoned Robert. We met over a meal and arranged to meet at the chalet next morning.

Together we looked at the décor which was a mixture of 'new old' and genuine old, mountain chalet. On the whole it was good, the ambience was a feel of a real mountain dwelling, but it was dark, almost too dark to read by, and the furnishings were appalling. I decided to have all new curtains, new modern sofas and chairs, and I would also look for a new dining table with matching chairs. The lighting too would all be updated with LED down lighters. Robert took notes for the decorators and I would see to all the furnishings in Paris. The beds would do, they were all good, but I would replace all the bedding. I asked Robert to dispose of all the too chintzy bed linen. The bunk beds for the children were awful. By taking in a storage cupboard, we could enlarge their room to have three single beds.

I spent the afternoon alone, taking measurements for the new furnishings. I ate alone in the hotel, surrounded by doubtful looking Russians two of whom attempted to flirt with me. I was politely cold, haughty, saying I was on business and preoccupied. They sloped off to the bar, but continued to watch as I ate.

In the morning I walked up the valley to the Saulire, a steep and winding path. It was a fine morning, the air was pure and the visibility good. Patches of old snow still nestled in the hollows on this north-facing slope looking dirty and sad. I surveyed the views from the top. On one side I could see down the sunbathed slope to Meribel and beyond, snow capped mountains shining in the sun. On the other, I could see the Courchevels, and way across the valley where the snow had retreated to the pinnacles of the mountains. In the afternoon I packed and set off for Paris, full of new Ideas. I drove all the way with just a short comfort stop. It was the longest time I had been alone for years.

I had new projects in mind, and that was the best thing, new challenges to take my mind off my troubles. I decided on the road that Paul Morel would get whatever was coming to him. Treachery like his could not be countenanced. I rang Franco from my stop.

'Franco, I want Paul shamed, not hurt physically. I want him in the gutter. If he finds a way to crawl out of it, then that will be his right, but at this time, I want him ruined. Can you do that?'

'I think so Madame. There are ways. Rest assured, your affairs will not feature in his downfall.'

Next day at the Maison, I gathered Jacques, Thomas and Nicole in the office, and put to them the idea for leather goods. I asked if they knew of a bag designer. Jacques offered a name, but said there was no chance of attracting him. Thomas mentioned someone who had been in the same year at fashion-college in London. He agreed to ring her to see whether she was available. I briefed him on what to say, that I would be interested in speaking to her, and I would travel to London to see her. I could also see my parents at the same time.

Wally appeared and I acquainted him with my plans. He was all in favour, enthusiastic for another line. With bags, he thought, the Beauvonne collection would be complete.

'So how are you Trudi,' he asked.

'I have emerged from my dark pit Wally. I'm sorry for falling apart. Now I feel rather ashamed but, Simon was not just my husband, he was my lover, he made me, he saved me from masculinity. He was all things to me. I realise now, that if it had not been the police causing his attack, it could have happened at any time, even when we made love or rode our horses.'

'And what of the children?'

'The children and the estate. That matter should be resolved soon. I have made representations to Monsieur Paul Morel, and the judgement against me will I am told be withdrawn. It will have cost me some money, but that is all.'

He looked at me with his trademark quizzical sideways glance. 'I know you well Trudi, it will not be that simple will it.'

'My life is never simple, as you say Wally. But you know, I do not like having enemies, especially powerful ones. You remember dirty David, the tennis coach at school of course. Well I don't do that sort of thing anymore.'

'I am glad that I am not Paul Morel.'

'Oh he is of no consequence. He was doing his job as the children's guardian but he was just misguided. No Wally, all will soon be resolved. Lawfully via the court.'

'Well, you know, you have my support.'

'Thank you Wally. By the way, when did you last go to London?'

'It is now two months. Yes Trudi, you are right. It is easy to forget our home nation when there are places like Shanghai, Dubai and Los Angeles.'

'I am going there looking for a handbag designer. I have a name, but if she is not willing, then I will go to the colleges to look for a likely recruit. Perhaps you and Sabine would like to accompany me. It would be good to have your support, and a trip for Sabine who is such a support for me. She could shop, we could see a show, take two or three days. Would you be agreeable?'

'Great idea and I could take her to meet my family, that is long overdue.'

'Then as soon as this young lady replies, we will plan to depart. In the mean time, there is much to do here Wally. We are now a young team. Our average age is twenty-eight. I want this house to be the trendsetters of Parisian fashion. In haute couture we are going to be radical, setting trends not spying on our competitors and following. Beauvonne is going to be more successful than Simon ever dreamed it could be. I have seven months before I resume my medical studies, to chart a course and I need the undivided support of everyone. Wally I am speaking to you now as I will speak to all the management. I want ideas from you all. I don't promise to use them all but we must all contribute.'

'You are back Comtesse Trudi, aren't you. If the sixth form could only see you now. Remember all those silly girls teasing you? It seems another World as I look at you now. Right, I will get cracking.'

Over the next few days I spent time with all the management, from the seamstresses upwards. Nicole had booked Champ de Mars at the Tour Eiffel for the next three shows. She also augmented the guest list with more A and B listers, chain store buyers and directors of companies as well as the press of three continents. We also planned a show for London and Rome, New York and Shanghai. For the first time ever, we would have a show in Dubai and Wally suggested that Los Angeles and Brasilia or Buenos Aires could now be worthwhile. He would fly there and find out which would be best.

Nicole managed to get stories of Beauvonne in important magazines and a story of the Curse in the London Times magazine and Time magazine in the US. We were firing on all cylinders.

I invited any member of staff, however junior to drop in to my office when the door was open. Closed it meant I was already seeing someone. Not many came to see me. One morning there was a knock and I looked up from going through some accounts to find Jean Rosier standing diffidently. He was a rather handsome lad, a trainee cutter who had been with us just five months.

'Oui Jean. What can I do for you?'

'Madame Trudi, I was reading Vogue last night and I came across Dior stockings. I wondered whether you had thought of stockings and tights. Designer named tights are higher quality, so cost more, I know because my mother likes to buy them; but I think the price to us cannot be so much more than the chain store lines. I thought it would be worth looking into.'

'Of course Jean. It is a good idea. I will ask someone, no Jean take that desk over there and research it. I suggest you use the reference book for manufacturers and make some enquiries. We want to know a range of prices don't we, for plain and patterned, see if there are different prices for colours. I leave it to you. If you have any ideas for designs, then I would be interested to see them. Write it out and let me have it when you are finished. Good, thank you Jean.'

Time went quickly. I was on edge all the time wondering how the negotiation with Paul had worked out. I knew that the minute there was news, Franco would phone me. I was impatient.

Days passed. At last I picked up the phone and heard Franco's gruff tones. 'Perhaps you would like to come for dinner Madame with your friend.'

'We will come tonight Franco if convenient.'

'Good Madame. At nine?'

'Excellent.'

I checked with Nicole and she was free. Franco's when we pushed through the frosted glass door, was full. Franco showed us to a secluded table, laid for four. He seated us and provided menus. He returned with a carafe of water accompanied by a man of around fifty.

'Madame, may I introduce the lawyer, Monsieur Di Pasqua. He will tell you what is happening.'

I looked him over. He was highly polished, a smart well fitting suit, shirt cuffs sporting expensive cuff links. His dark hair was thinning and plastered to his skull. He wore rimless spectacles that reminded me of photos I had seen of Glen Miller the band leader. He smiled as we shook hands.

We sat down. 'May I speak Madame?' He meant in front of Nicole.

'Oh yes, please.'

'Very well Madame. I have seen Morel and he is prepared to settle for the sum you have given us. There will be a hearing but the judge is sympathetic and Morel will give evidence in your favour. You do not have to attend. That takes place next week. Morel knows now that he was very wrong in taking away your rights.'

'That is very good news. Thank you.'

'In seven days time you will be at liberty to live in the Chateau and be the children's sole guardian. I need your naturalisation papers for the court.'

'Of course. Do I send them to you?'

'I will collect them from your villa Madame, tomorrow morning at 8.30.'

'I will have them ready Monsieur Di Pasqua.'

'As regards the future Madame, all will be taken care of. Morel will not trouble you again.'

'That is very good to know, thank you. It is a great relief to know that I am fully in command of everything again.'

'I will leave you to your meal young ladies. Eight-thirty tomorrow then Madame.'

He took my hand and squeezed it. He did the same with Nicole's hand. He left via Franco's private area behind the curtained doorway.

'Trudi, that was creepy. Who was he?'

'A lawyer.'

'But why meet here?'

'He is a friend of Franco, but very discreet and reliable.'

Franco appeared before Nicole could question me further. I was elated that everything was on track, and would take much less time than I had thought. This lawyer must have powerful friends.

We ate escalope of veal Marsala, very rich and good. We walked home arm in arm.

As we parted in the villa, Nicole said, 'Trudi, be very careful with this lawyer. I shall have a nightmare.'

'He is highly recommended by Franco. You heard him, all is resolved.'

'He probably used thumb screws.'

'I think he may have used persuasion, but Paul proved to be a snake. I am not bothered about Paul. He must accept that reward for a crime, may not always be what he wants.'

'OK. I hope all will be well. I understand you are making a visit to London. I would also like to go, to talk to the London fashion magazines. I have ten contacts there I ought to see. And Trudi, I would like to make a press release about your visit and have photos of you arriving and during the stay, and photos of our team and reason for the visit. It is such a good marketing opportunity, your return to the country of your birth etc. Of course, they will dig up your past too. Can you live with that?'

'I think I have to put up with it. If I am to remain in the public eye, and I am certainly not going to become a recluse, then there is no escaping my past. Yes of course you should come and do what we pay you for, Nicole. I should have asked you. I wonder whether we should not throw a dinner for the people we want to meet. Wally has three buyers from the top stores and our boutique manager from the Bond Street store. I have a potential recruit to see, a bag designer and you have all your contacts. I will phone around and find a hotel and restaurant.'

I phoned around. It was surprising how busy the better hotels were. I ended booking a room for Thomas and Nicole and Wally and Sabine and for me in the Café Royal, for three nights. I also booked tables, for three nights, the middle night would include all our London contacts, fashion Press and our shop contacts and hopefully a new recruit. I briefed everyone that this was a working visit, so they had better arrange appointments and invite their contacts to the dinner.

I went to see Jacques, to tell him of the London expedition. It occurred to me that he could feel left out and I did not want to upset our haute couture designer.

He jumped at the opportunity to go to London, but it would be good for our contacts to meet the whole team, especially the designer of the prestige end of the market.

We now had a list of applicants for position of accountant. I have never liked accountants, they very often see the difficulties and how to save money rather than the need to invest and branch out. They are the antithesis of entrepreneurship. However, it would be, and had been in most of Simon's time, irresponsible to be without someone to keep an eye on our finances, especially as Beauvonne was growing and diversifying.

I asked Wally and Nicole to go through the applications with me. Eventually we had fifteen possibles which by agreement we cut to eight probables. We sent emails inviting them to attend in two days time.

The Maison was a hive of industry. An agency was providing the models, but we still had to vet them to see that they suited us, and the clothes were assigned to specific models with their varying assets in mind. It was a huge task with which I had never been involved except as a rather minor model.

Jacques and Thomas asked if I was willing to model four designs. When I saw them, I had to agree. The first dress was a romantic tea into evening dress, a fitted bodice, and dreamy diaphanous skirt, ending four inches above the knee. It came in a black version which made it more evening wear with black bead embroidery on the bodice and a white version with a slightly longer skirt and no embellishment. I chose to wear the black one at the end of the haute couture daywear part of the show. The other was a business suit, loose fitting trousers but tight on the ankle with a jacket that swept across the body to fix over the hip, accentuating bust and waist. It was a showstopper. I decided to wear that first.

Thomas for evening wear had designed a ladies evening trouser suit, similar to the one I would wear as a day suit, but black, satin silk and the trousers were only just opaque. I would wear that at the end of the ready-made show.

Lastly there was a trumpet dress, the foot of the skirt lying in a pool circling the feet, darkest green silk. I would wear that at the finale when I thanked everyone. This time there would be more dogs and we had to make sure that they were all socialised. One model had volunteered her cat, on a lead. We would have to see. Anything to catch the headlines and I could see Sheba my Arab mare making an appearance if the animal gimmick persisted.

It occurred to me in that minute that we ought to have watches and jewellery too. I would look into that for next time. I knew there was an Italian watchmaker using Swiss movements, putting bespoke cases on watches.

Wally had suggested men's underwear. Pants at £20 a time, there must be profit in it and male underwear was a much simpler market than women's.

Wally, Nicole and I did the interviews for accountant. Even though we had weeded them, it was disappointing. In the end we had two outstanding candidates, a forty six year old who had worked for a train company and a young woman of thirty, who had come up the hard way and had been working in one of the global accountancy firms. I chose her and managed to convince Wally and Nicole that she would fit better with our young team. I phoned her with the news and gave her a starting date after our London visit.

Di Pasqua phoned to say that the court had found in my favour. The papers were on the way to me in the post. I could now resume my life at the Chateau with the children. It was great news.

I decided to throw a party for the management and domestic staff at the Chateau over the weekend, Thomas and Nicole, Jacques and his partner, Wally and Sabine, Sophie and Laurent, Sabine's parents, Élise and Jean Luc, Franco and his family.

Chapter 6.

Thursday, I took off for the Chateau to arrange everything and to see the children at last. I just hoped they remembered me.

As I drove, I had butterflies in my stomach. The children were still so young, 3 years and two, they may have forgotten me already. I suspected that little Sebastian would not remember me anyway. I cursed Paul for his greed and using the children as a lever.

Driving my Mercedes tourer convertible was more pleasant than driving Simon's huge saloon that I had sold to pay Paul. I did not miss that at all, but regretted the reason for the sale. Well, that was done with. He was paid and I was shot of him, legally French and legally in possession of the Chateau and the children as Simon had wished. That was all that mattered now, and getting back to normal.

I rolled to a stop in front of the Chateau, pulled my bags from the back seat and bounded up the steps. I pushed at the door and it opened to my touch. I was home. Memories of Simon flooded back and I almost choked as I entered the vestibule. I dropped my bags and turned to the salon door as I heard the pound of tiny feet. André came through the door first, followed by a more timid Adèle. I knelt down and André nearly knocked me over as he flung himself upon me, then Adèle followed his example and Sébastien squeezed in amongst us. I rolled over with the weight of them and they took this as a game and rolled on top. I looked up to see Sophie's smiling face. She helped me to my feet and we too embraced.

'It is good to have you home Trudi, so good.'

'It is good to be home Sophie and to see you and the children. Nicole has kept me up to date, but, I can hardly believe the nightmare is over.'

'That man, he only came here twice. He did not look at the children. What did he want Trudi?'

'Money. I have had to pay him. I could have waited months for the courts to decide without his cooperation, so I paid him off. It is a lesson for me not to trust people I don't know. Anyway Sophie, we are having a coming home party this weekend. So ask Laurent if you will and his parents. Wally and Sabine will be here, Thomas and your sister, Jean Luc and Élise, Jacques and his partner and Franco, his wife and three children. You know Sophie, Nicole has been my constant support. She has been so good. All my girls are just excellent.

'Hey André, what are you doing?' He was under my skirt. He came out chuckling, still holding the hem.

'Anyway Sophie, I better go and see the cook. Is everything all right in the household?'

'Yes Trudi, the housekeeper has been more difficult than she normally is, but perhaps that is understandable. There has been so much uncertainty.'

'I will see what is to be done. We will have to give her a hand getting rooms ready. Can you help with that? If we do it together, it will be so much easier with those big beds.'

I went to the kitchen. Gustave the cook and Hortense the housekeeper were there. I embraced them both.

'Gustave, I want to have a party this weekend, Saturday night. And you are both invited with your families. I should ask someone from outside to do the food, so that you can enjoy yourself. Will you mind that? It is very short notice, but I did not win the court case until yesterday. So what do you say? Who do we know could do the food?'

'I do not know Madame. Out here in the country, we do not know about such things.

'Then we will have to do it ourselves. Let us draw up a menu. What about Lobster bisque? We can do that?'

'I have lobsters in the freezer. We can make lobster salad if you buy some salad Madame, and we can use the shells to make a bisque, so we would have two starters. Then we could do racks of lamb as a main and apple Normande for pudding. I can phone for the racks and they will be here tomorrow. How many are we?'

'Your families, and eleven adults plus my children and three more.'

'It will be me and my wife. Hortense, who are you bringing.'

'My husband and my daughter.'

'So that is eighteen, let us say. Oh but I forgot, there is also Jean Luc and Élise and Jean Luc's parents. There are three other estate workers. I should ask them too. that will be nearly thirty. Can we do that?'

'I will ask my wife to come in to help,' Gustave said, 'but Madame, you will have to go shopping and I don't think I can cook for you tomorrow. Perhaps you will eat out, that will give us a chance to prepare everything.'

'Make me a list and I will shop. I will take Sophie and the children to Lisieux. Now I must try and see people to invite them.'

I made my way round to Sabine. We embraced. I did not tell her the whole story, it would keep. She agreed to ask the estate workers to the party and her family as well.

I returned to the Chateau. Gustave had the list of shopping. Sophie and I dressed the children and we piled into the Land Rover. We were soon in Lisieux . We ate at Rive Gauche, a short mealtime because we needed to go to the market and the wholesalers.

The market provided all the fresh food, vegetables and fruit, cheese, bread and some herbs Gustave needed. We bought the rest at the wholesalers, a case of champagne, a good red wine and a white so that we would not deplete the Chateau cellar too much, and two kilos of our usual coffee. On the way home Sophie had the children singing the new songs she had taught them. We carried the food into the kitchen, the children carrying little parcels, expressions of effort on their lovely faces.

After tea, Sophie and I put the children to bed. I spent the evening going through my wardrobe to thin it out. There were items that reminded me too much of Simon, which I knew I could not wear again because they would make me sad. There were some that I did not want to wear again. I decided to put them all on hangers and the guests could help themselves if they fancied any of them. It was the best day I'd had for a long time.

Next day we all busied ourselves with party preparations. Gustave and his wife made appetizers. They involved the children, teaching them how to cut out the pastry in tiny rounds and squares. They were also allowed to mix the ingredients, pouring ingredients into the mixing bowl and watching as the machine did the work. Adèle was taught to weigh the ingredients, her quick mind already knowing her numbers. She was also very bossy with André, who wanted to be approximate.

After an hour they'd had enough and so had Gustave. I took them up to change into their riding clothes and we went to see their ponies. I led the twins and Sophie led Sébastien on his pony. André wanted to kick his on and go faster, but a sharp word from me brought him into line.

Sébastien was still uncertain of me, preferring Sophie, but taking his lead from the twins began reacting to me as they did in a sort of puzzled way. I knew I would have to pay him extra attention for him to bond with me again.

Back at the Chateau we commenced making the beds to Hortense's direction. We involved the children, they thinking it some sort of game. That finished we went down to the salon. The day turned dull, drizzle drifting in from the west. Sophie and I settled down to play and educate the children, reading with them, playing counting games and turning the toy clock and rewarding them with a sweet when they told us the time. I managed to tempt Sébastien to sit on my knee as I sat on the floor, showing him the pictures in various books. I found that the children were all quite advanced for their age, Adèle was already reading and André recognised letters and one or two words. Sophie had done a good job while I was banished.

As we bathed them I asked Sophie if she was still happy. She was reassuring. She was still seeing Laurent, Sabine's younger brother who farmed with his father, Simon's cousin. This relationship made living in rural Normandy worthwhile, especially as she now had a car for her own use. It was a great relief to find her happy and settled.

Work had stopped in the kitchen. Gustave and his wife had gone to their estate cottage. I made a snack for Sophie and I. We had just finished when Nicole, Thomas, Élise and Jean Luc arrived. Wally arrived with Sabine, pleased to stay at the Chateau rather than with Sabine's family for a change. I bunged three pizzas in the oven and produced some of the cheap champagne I had bought yesterday. We had rather a merry evening.

Happy as I was, there was an emptiness, part of me missing, because Simon was not there. I had never been at the Chateau without him until the week after his death and again now. I missed him dreadfully. He had been my anchor, given me a reason for living, affirmed who I was and given me legitimacy as mistress of Beauvonne. Now I was here in my own right, yet I felt as though I was merely a pretender. We played a game of charades and I felt terribly insecure, stumbling over my answers.

Wally gave me one of his quizzical looks. It was like going back eight years to schooldays, when I had mostly been confident, exhilarated by being who I wanted to be at last, but at times losing all confidence in my new persona when something disturbed by equilibrium.

We finished the game. Wally asked if he could have a word about work.

'We better go to the study Wally, if you'll excuse us everyone.' I said.

The study was snug and restful after the noise of the salon.

'What's up?' he asked after he had closed the door.

'What Wally?'

'You, the confident Comtesse, you nearly went to pieces in there. What's happened.'

'Just being here Wally. Before I was just an appendage of Simon, here because he wanted me to be. I suddenly felt as though I had no right to his legacy. I just lost confidence in being here, my whole journey. I crisis of confidence in who I am versus where I have come from.'

'But your position is the same as that of any widow who's husband has left them the estate. Of course you deserve to be here. After *all* you have done for Beauvonne and what you have been through? I should think so.'

'I know all that. You have known me longer than anyone else here, in all my different personas. Sometimes I just feel like an actor, acting a part. My psyche is not anchored like yours or Sabine's. When I am busy, I mean really busy, pushed, like in the hospital and running around after Simon and the children, I do not have time to turn inward and self-examining. I have had a good day. Yesterday too, was a good day, being back here, with *my* children. Then suddenly I missed Simon. I did not feel worthy of being left all this as a legacy.'

'Did you not carry Beauvonne when he was ill? Have you not produced so many ideas and appointments to get us where we are today. What would have happened to Beauvonne, if you had not picked up the reins and driven it forward. You know Simon thought the world of you, and he was right to. He was a pleasant man, astute, a gentleman and well mannered. An aristocrat in the best sense of the word, but he did not have your drive, ambition and vision. Without you, Beauvonne would have remained just a rather sleepy haute couture house, slowly dropping behind the opposition. He was too much the aristocrat. Come on Trudi, you know all this.'

'I know, you are right. But there is also my sexuality, a main cause of insecurity, especially after what Paul said to me.'

'What did he say?'

'That I was not a real woman, that kissing me revolted him. Even though by the time he said that I knew he was a bastard, it really hurt. Destroyed my confidence in, well who I am.'

'So that's it. That's what he said.' He laughed, more a chuckle than a guffaw. 'I can tell you, that I have often wondered what it would be like to kiss you, but you have seemed as remote from me as well, Kate, Duchess of Cambridge or I don't know who, Jennifer Anniston for example even though I met her in Los Angeles. But I have thought about it, and yes, fancied you. When you walked into the school restaurant that first evening as Trudi, I can tell you, there was a stirring in my loins. Peter said he would, well to use his term, 'give you one! Then there was Stuart and Dirty David. For Christ's sake, don't you see how everyone looks up to you?'

'You sound like Simon. He told me off about my insecurity.'

'Good. He should have given you a good spanking if you came out with the same stuff as this. Come we should get back.'

He grasped me and kissed me, hard on the lips, then relaxed and softly. I did not resist. I had always wondered what it would be like kissing him too.

'I can tell you, that was all right for me Trudi la Comtesse de Beauvonne. Not a word to Sabine though.'

'Of course not. I enjoyed it, but I love you and Sabine, so never again Wally.'

'Proved a point though, didn't it?'

Chapter 7.

I did not go to sleep readily that night. Wally had been my hero at school, a boy and later a young man of fairness and discretion. I had always been fond of him, though at school I was not equipped to do anything about it. As head boy and girl, it had been like a sort of marriage, and I have to confess that I had girlish imaginings of being his wife.

His kindness in the evening and that kiss troubled me. It had aroused feelings that I had buried. Sabine was now his fiancée and she was very dear to me, so I could do nothing about my feelings. I hoped someone else would come along eventually to replace Simon and my long harboured yearning for Wally. I think Simon had been aware of my liking of Wally. He had joked about it once or twice. However, at that time I had thought of Wally as a boy in contrast to Simon who was certainly a man. Now Wally was certainly a man and in a way, the alpha male in my family.

I got up and took a sleeping pill. I was asleep in a few minutes.

I awoke just after seven and lay thinking about the day ahead. Wally and his kiss had faded. I poked the imagery of that kiss and his arms about me back into a dark recess of my mind. I would find someone to love. I had no doubt. I was, even with my history an attractive proposition. Wealthy, attractive and successful, there would be men who could ignore the tragedy of my birth as a male.

I got up and dressed, new matching underwear, silk and very pretty. A day dress, a shirtwaister in silk dupion and new square-toed five inch heals to match. I did my hair carefully, letting it fall in waves to its full length. I decided to ring Professeur Rousse, a father figure at the hospital, to see whether he would like to come for the party and stay the night. It would be good to keep in touch if I really intended to go back to my medical studies.

I could hear the children before I reached the nursery. As I approached Sophie emerged laughing.

The children were trailing behind her, giggling.

'What are you all so happy about?' I asked.

'They were plotting to jump on Maman and wake you up, but you must have known. Trudi, you are very beautiful today, exceptional.'

'Thank you Sophie, and you too. Sophie, we are not the same size, it is a pity, because I am turning out a lot of clothes. Before I take them to a dealer or the poor, you can see if anything suits you. I want to bring it all down to the music room for people to see and choose. Will you help me after breakfast?'

'Bien sûr. The children can help too.'

'And while I think about it Sophie, we have a music room but no one plays. I think we should give the children some music lessons. Can you find a teacher locally?'

'I will try. I will ask Laurent's mother, she may know someone.'

'Good. Then we have also to get ready for tonight. Everyone can help, guests as well, don't you think?'

'Of course Trudi.'

The day passed quickly. The work was done with everyone helping. There was a brilliant atmosphere of bonhomie. We ate mussels and chips for lunch with Gewûrztraminer from Alsace. Nicole informed me, it came from a vineyard not far from their home.

In the afternoon I recruited a working party to set the table and to assist Gustave in the kitchen. Everything was ready by five. Franco and his family arrived just after, larger than life, he and his wife making a great fuss of us all. One would have thought it was a party of fifteen arriving not two adults and three children. The vestibule echoed with the children's gasps at the ornate ceiling and walls. I showed them to their two rooms, his three children sharing a king size bed in a room adjacent to Franco. As I descended the stairs, Professeur Rousse entered, a big black hat upon his head and his spectacles steaming up from the night air. His wife was quite petite, one of those bird like women, with a fine boned sharp but pleasant face. I showed them up to their room and confirmed the arrangements for the evening.

Dinner was at seven-thirty. I was allowing the children on this special occasion to stay up. They had slept in the afternoon while we were busy, so they would be fresh for the evening. Sophie was as usual efficient and had managed them well. Together we laid out their clothes and Nicole was recruited to assist in dressing them. I went to my room and selected my dress carefully. I decided on a long dress with a plunging back, V neck, with slashed three quarter sleeves and brush train in French blue silk shantung. I had to tape myself, and I thought of all the times Simon had delighted in doing that for me. I put my hair up, with Sabine's help, Helen of Troy style, piled in plaits upon my head. She was surprisingly good with hair.

I gathered the children from the nursery. They appeared impeccably dressed, happy and full of mischief. and accompanied by Tasha we descended. Rousse was already down, sitting comfortably and talking to Wally. I guessed they were discussing me by the way they looked. I did not mind, they were I knew both my good friends.

Sabine's parents and Laurent arrived and then the rest drifted down, Nicole and I fetched in the canapés and Wally and Jean Luc opened bottles of champagne. The estate workers including Jean Luc's parents, and Gustave and his wife and Hortense and her husband and daughter came through. Everyone mingled, staff and friends. Rousse was very jolly, much to the consternation of his wife who kept shushing him and telling him to slow down. The children gambolled and followed Franco's three, playing hide and seek around the throng and behind the furniture and curtains. Sophie kept them in check.

It was hard work. I sat everyone down and we girls were waitresses bringing in the soup accompanied by plates of pain de compagne.

The boys then cleared the plates and we brought in the lobster salad. Gustave went out to manage the portions of rack of lamb with Normandy new potatoes and creamed spinach.

Again we girls were waitresses. The food was delicious, the lamb succulent and so tasty. The twins and Sébastien were on their pudding while everyone had a little break. When they finished, it was off to bed for them and they said bonne nuit most charmingly. We tucked them up and came down for pudding. Gustave brought it in and served it with cream and ice cream at the table. It was excellent.

When everyone had finished. I tapped my glass and stood.

'I just want to say a few words. I wanted you all here, all my great friends and supporters, who have helped me so much over the years and especially the last few months since the death of dear Simon. This is not a thank you feast, but a celebration of Beauvonne and its friends. I hope that I will make us all better off than we have been, especially the Beauvonne estate staff who work so hard and sometimes have been taken for granted. I want to get to know you all better and you must feel free to come to me at any time.

'There are extra special people here. Sophie, who has looked after my children so well. Nicole her sister who has propped me up these last months and who works so hard for Beauvonne. Sabine, who is transforming the Beauvonne estate, making it more profitable and attractive too. Her good work will be reflected in bonuses to the estate staff too. I want to thank everyone at Maison Beauvonne. We are making it a premier league fashion house. And Professeur Rousse who has been so kind to me at Pitié Salpêtrière. Thank you all for your love, your help and understanding. I hope you have enjoyed this little feast.'

Rousse was hammering on the table as others clapped. He rose to his feet.

'I do not know any of you, except our hostess. I am her Professeur at the hospital and it is my hope that Trudi le modèle will return to her medical studies because she will be an exceptional médicin. I say le modèle because when we first met, I did not think her serious. She had taken time off and without knowing the reason, I condemned her. At that time, all I knew was what I had read in the newspapers. How wrong I was. Trudi is a serious and diligent young woman as well as being beautiful and a little notorious if one reads the gutter press. I am very pleased to know her and to be counted as a friend. A toast to Trudi and Friendship.'

I blushed and I cried. I bit my lip and managed to pull myself together as they raised their glasses.

'That is enough, but thank you Professeur. This is a meal for friends. I need everyone of you. Bless you all.'

I rose and started to clear plates. Everyone joined in and we soon had coffee, brandy and liqueurs on the table. I circulated, paying special attention to the estate and Chateau workers who I did not know well. No one wanted to depart and people were still talking at two o'clock. Rousse was very witty and made everyone laugh with his stories of the hospital. Gustave was surprisingly friendly. I had good people around me. I was so lucky. They slowly departed to their homes or their rooms. Sabine kissed me and departed, leaving Wally and I last. We locked the doors and checked the windows. We climbed the stairs together. He kissed me at my door and I wished he hadn't.

Chapter 8.

Sunday and we all relaxed. Gustave was back in his kitchen providing us all with food. I thanked him for yesterday. He was warmer to me than he had ever been before. Even the difficult Hortense had been pleasant yesterday evening. She never appeared on a Sunday, being a good old school Catholic, she observed the Sabbath.

I escorted Rousse and his wife on a short tour of the estate. We walked down to Sabine's new lake, which had now started to merge into the countryside and look as though it had always been there. She had created a vista, planting trees protected by wrought iron fences around which the sheep grazed. We walked the formal garden and round to the stables. Madame Rousse knew horses and loved Arabians, so she was captivated by Sheba.

My guests lazed. We ate cold meats and salad for lunch then people departed. I seemed to spend the afternoon kissing and hugging and waving from the front steps. Soon there was only me, Sophie and the children left.

'I think we should all go to Paris Sophie. Is that agreeable?'

'Of course. I will get the children's clothes packed and mine. I'll phone Laurent to let him know. Perhaps he could come and stay a night or two in Paris?'

'Whatever you want Sophie. He is welcome. I should invite his parents at some time too. I do want to be on good terms with Simon's family.'

'Laurent's mother is very kind. His father is a bit gruff, but he is all right really. He did not like Simon, you know, I think jealous. However he has said kind things since his death, so perhaps all is well now.'

'Well I hope so. I want a happy family.'

'Do you know Trudi you amaze me. Sometimes you are the most hard-bitten business woman, efficient, smart and clever. Then you say things like that, as though you are a little girl, innocent and loving, untouched by the bad in the World.'

'I think that is a nice compliment Sophie. Let's pack for Paris, then we can relax.'

Next day in Paris I made straight for the Maison while Sophie drove to the villa. Wally was preparing to go to Dubai and then on to the Far East. Nicole was busy with London appointments, her own and under Wally's direction, making appointments for him too. London was in two weeks time, so we had time to plan that properly and we had a lot of other work for the next show to complete.

I went to see Wally before he took a taxi to the airport.

'Everything under control Wally? Nothing we should discuss before you go?'

'No everything is fine, pretty straight forward these visits now. The designers brief is very detailed and the new lines should go down well. I won't let you down.'

'I know you won't Wally. And is everything OK with you and Sabine? The wedding is still nine months away, but one has to think about things.'

He responded with a quizzical look as usual when he was a little uncomfortable. 'Now what are you fishing for?'

'I don't know. I just wonder. As an engaged couple, you seem more like an old married couple.'

'Nice. Because we are not always kissing and holding hands? Sabine is lovely but not romantic like that.'

'And are you romantic like that? I know with Simon, we just wanted to touch each other all the time. Even after we were married, my heart beat faster when I was going to meet him or as I returned from work knowing he was there to welcome me. Is it like that for you?'

'No, not like that. It is good, but not exciting. Should it be still? We are not teenagers.'

'Yes Wally, I think it should still be like that. I do not want to see two of my best friends make a mistake. It is my dream to see you as a married couple, but it has to be right.'

'Why are you saying this?'

'I introduced you to each other. I gave Sabine a makeover, from countrywoman to a sophisticated beauty, to trap you. I could never forgive myself if this did not work out.'

'Ah Madame Machiavelli again.' He kissed me on the cheek. 'I have a lot of flying hours to think about this. Never fear, I shall not hurt Sabine. It will be OK. Anyway, I better go, the taxi will be waiting.'

'Bon voyage Wally et bonne chance.'

'Et tu Trudi de Beauvonne, notre Princesse. Take care.'

I reflected after he had gone. Had I said too much? Well I had to say something. He had not seemed annoyed or defensive, but if there was any doubt at all, I could not bear my match making to end badly, especially for two such friends.

The week passed quickly. I followed Wally's progress via his emailed orders and requests. At the weekend we went to the Chateau. Wally was in Shanghai.

I rode Sheba both days and Sabine and I took the children out on their ponies on leading reins. They managed very well and it brought home to me how starting such things in early life made learning so much easier.

After we had stabled the ponies and Sophie had taken the children for their lunch, I asked Sabine whether she had heard form Wally. She said there was one phone call from Dubai, then nothing. I moved to other subjects. I asked how she occupied herself while Wally was away. She told me that her family had a wide circle of friends, so she saw them and sometimes went to local farming meetings and swapped notes.

We entered her office and she switched on the electric fire. The day had turned cool, a sea mist had rolled in and the temperature had dropped several degrees. She made hot chocolate in her little machine. We settled in the two armchairs beside her fire.

'Luxury isn't it? Don't worry Trudi. I keep busy. I am not sitting pining for as you say, my undemonstrative Englishman.'

'Oh good. I did not like thinking of your being lonely. And is he still undemonstrative?'

'Oh Trudi. You should not worry so much.'

'I worry about all my family. I can't help it.'

'Trudi, everything is all right. Do not think about us. We are adults you know. Look the marriage will not take place for months, until our house has been renovated completely. Wally and I are not so happy at the moment, but we have time. We do not argue, it is just that we are both busy and tired.'

'And I am partly responsible for that.'

"No Trudi, you could not do other than you have, in fact Wally and I think you have been remarkable. Yes, you broke down, but then who would not in your place.'

'I will say no more. It is not my business except that I love you both. And you are happy with your position as estate manager still?'

'Oh yes, very happy. It makes my father both mad and proud, proud that I can do this and mad because he thinks women are wives and mothers first but might make a little pin money, and the Estate is three times the size of our family farm. And you know, he has always been jealous of the Chartrands of Beauvonne. That is what all the trouble has been, going back to Simon's father who was my grandfather's brother.'

'Well I guessed as much, though I never discussed this with Simon. I just knew there were problems and said Simon should make an effort to make it up to his cousin. He did try.'

'Oh by the end, I think they were fine and father broke down when he heard of Simon's death. And he wishes you well too. He is very old fashioned sitting out here in rural France, but you have won him over.'

'I am glad Sabine, especially for the children growing up. They are Chartrands, your relatives. It is important for the different branches of the family to stay together.'

'Oh Trudi, you are so sweet sometimes. You would have everyone kissing and holding hands.'

'I have learnt in my life, that most problems can be overcome and those one cannot solve, should be left alone. Yes, I want to live in a place where people are nice to each other, especially families.'

'Will you look for another man?'

'That is a big question. Why do you ask?' I was suddenly feeling guilty and vulnerable.

'Well you are still very young and beautiful, rich and talented. I would think there are men out there who would throw themselves at you.'

'It would have to be someone special Sabine. You know that.'

I looked her in the face. She was smiling mischievously. 'What about Wally?'

'What makes you ask that. He is engaged to you.'

'But if you had not been with Simon, Wally would have been on your list for a partner, wouldn't he?'

'I have a strange relationship with Wally. He was a bit like a brother at school, even before I changed, looking out for me, seeing off the bullies, but even more so after I became a girl. He was the one I could rely on, always. I had dreams of marrying the brother of a girl friend, but he was five years older, which matters a lot when one is sixteen or seventeen. Yes, my heart beat faster when Wally was sweet to me at school. He was big and handsome, true and nice. Boys are not very nice at that age, nor girls for that matter. I had a lot of petty bullying, skirt lifting, trying to pull my knickers down, that sort of constant harassment He could stop it with a look. When he appeared as a candidate to work for Beauvonne, it took my breath away. One can have romantic thoughts, but not actually do anything about it, can't one? And there was Simon who had done so much for me and who I loved and admired.'

'And now?'

'Now I have too much else to think about. My Beauvonne family, that is everyone connected to me, you, Sophie, the Estate workers, though that is in your good hands, everyone at Maison Beauvonne and getting back to my studies. A lover or another husband? No I do not think so, not at the moment, perhaps never. Simon was so special to me. He picked me up, paid for surgery, he and another friend, sorted out my medication. It all bound me to him emotionally. I do not know quite where I am sexually. As a teenager I had a lesbian lover, Ellie, Eleanor. I was too uncertain of myself to appreciate her then, and I hardly see her except when she reports from some war zone.

'Marriage is not everything you know, and to be truthful, sex, making love means hardly anything at all to me unless it means giving my partner pleasure. With Simon, it was good. He was exciting and ingenious. I do not imagine another man could replace him that way.'

'So no one else could give you a posy?'

'Did I tell you about that?'

'No, that modèle, La Poulette.'

'There can only be one posy. So if she knows, then everyone will know. Oh well, so what. I think it is rather funny, and I would rather have pansies than hair. I have panties to cover myself anyway, so why do I need hair.'

'I think that was genius, Trudi. It is nothing to be ashamed of is it?'

'I think we should talk about the estate or other people Sabine.' I stood, looking at her map of the Estate, the fields on it coloured in according to crop.

She swung me to her. I had not noticed how mesmerising her eyes could be nor how green they were. 'I love you Trudi. Thank you for your faith in me.' She kissed me full on the mouth.

'I love you too Sabine.'

'No Trudi. I really love you. If I were not with Wally, and if I thought I would have a chance with you, then I would be your slave. Now you can run away and sack me.'

I said nothing. I was too confused. I had never thought of having another lesbian affair. I was fond of women, liked their company more than that of men, but sex, that would be a very different thing. Yet with Ellie.....I confessed to myself that it had been fun, enjoyable and in her arms, I had felt desirable, valued and aroused. I had not given myself fully, because I was so repressed, shy, embarrassed by who I was.

I liked the power of men, liked being protected and desired. Women gave me a different sort of love. The security of the sisterhood, empathy, commonality, tenderness and fun.

'I think we have said too much, Sabine. But I still love you, like a sister. You, Nicole, Sophie, I think of us as sisters.'

I returned to the Chateau and made a snack. I ate it alone in the kitchen, a piece of pizza and some leftover salad. I was very disturbed by Sabine. How could she be with Wally if that was how she felt? How did I feel about both of them? I could not cope with it. I downed a glass of wine from an opened bottle. It was not very good, French burgundy at its worst. I guessed it was Gustave's cooking wine.

I found Sophie and the children. Sébastien was asleep on the couch and Sophie was reading quietly to the twins. It was one of the 'where is my' books, this one, Où est mon éléphant? The twins were entranced and giggling, curling up with pleasure at the unexpected. It was a joy to see. We read more books and did some drawing. It was soon teatime. I made their tea, beans on toast, an English import that they loved, followed by hot chocolate. We bathed them and put them to bed, The twins taught me a new song, 'Ah les crocodiles', clapping their hands and rocking. I kissed them all good night. How wonderful it was to feel their little arms about my neck. I wanted to cry, for being so close to them, I thought of dear Simon who I had to coax to be a more in touch father.

Sophie and I sat watching television. The news was not good, dead soldiers in Afghanistan, a new earthquake and miserable spring weather. We watched a film, 'Dances with Wolves' which we had not seen. It had some good moments. What struck me most was the vastness of the American plains and the loneliness and oppression of the ever-present danger. I went to bed feeling slightly oppressed myself. The film had failed to expunge the memory of Sabine's declaration. As I went through the ritual of makeup removal and washing, I could not get Wally or Sabine out of my mind. I had not taken a sleeping pill for some weeks. I took half a tablet and mercifully fell asleep. I knew I would think about that tomorrow though.

Another week of work before the London trip. Nicole had everything under control. All the contacts were lined up and the hotel had confirmed and the restaurant was booked. I spent much of the week with Nicole again and also preparing office space for our new accountant. We gathered all the financial reports and filed them in her office. I hoped she would know what to do, for I had no idea of accounting.

The evenings were spent baby-sitting while Sophie was out with Laurent. It was good to see them with time to themselves and enjoying each other's company. I had never said much to Laurent. He seemed a quiet young man, sober and self-contained, but Sophie assured me he was very funny.

On Thursday he and I chatted while waiting for Sophie to get ready to go out. He was very pleasant. When I mentioned Sabine, it was easy to see that he was a great admirer of his older sister.

'Are you looking forward to seeing her married?'

'Perhaps.'

'What do you mean?'

'I don't know if it will happen. I do not see that spark between them. I love my sister and Wally is a good man, but perhaps there is not enough magic.'

'And do you and Sophie have magic?'

He blushed and smiled, looking particularly boyish and more charming than I had ever seen him. 'I think so. She is a marvel with the children. She makes me very happy too.'

'So you are going to run off with my wonderful nanny. And I will have to find a wonderful wedding present for you too. It looks like a poor deal for me.'

'But not yet Trudi. We are young and anyway, she can work after we marry, at least until we have children of our own.'

'Well Laurent, when it happens, Beauvonne will supply your suit and all the dresses too, as an extra gift. And if you want to use the Chateau, you would be welcome to.'

'Thank you Trudi. That is a lovely offer.'

'We are family Laurent and Sophie is like a sister to me.' Sophie appeared. 'Have a good evening,' I said.

The weekend was spent in Paris as we were all going on the Eurostar Monday morning. It was very strange just Sophie, Laurent, the children and I in the villa. Jean Luc and Élise were working shifts at different hospitals and Nicole was with Thomas. I missed Nicole. I missed my medical friends and above all, on this sunny spring weekend, I missed Simon. We amused the children in the Tuileries, and bought lovely ice creams from a shop on Ile St Louis. Laurent played football with the children, making two trees in an avenue the goal posts. Sophie and I sat watching.

I was, as Sophie remarked, quiet. My spirits had suddenly dropped.

'You have triste,' she said, 'are you well enough to go to London?'

'Oui Sophie, I am missing Simon. This is the first big trip, an important one and I am missing Simon. He and I bought ice creams when I first came to Paris at this same shop. I was just eighteen. So much has happened since that time.'

'Of course you must be sad.' She took my arm. " You can do this Trudi. You are stronger than any of us. Don't worry about the children. I will look after them with Laurent. And my sister will look after you.'

'I know you will. And Nicole, I don't know what I would do without my little assistant, she is so much more. You are very talented girls, in different ways, but I love you both as though you really are my sisters. And Sabine too.'

'Ah Sabine.'

'Why do you say that?'

'Sabine and Wally. I do not think they are Josephine and Napoleon. I think Sabine is going through the motions, but she is tepid.'

'You must be wrong. She is going to London to meet his parents.'

'Trudi, she has never been to London.'

'That is why she is going? No, I think you are wrong.'

'Not the only reason. She does not love your friend Wally, I know. We have spent a lot of time together.'

'Then why are they planning a wedding?'

'I am going to say, but you must not be cross. I think she is in love with someone else.'

'Someone I know?'

'You do not know Trudi?'

'I am asking.'

'It is you Trudi. She worships you, don't you know?'

I blushed. For some unaccountable reason tears filled my eyes. I realised that Sabine was fond, like an elder sister at times, And just over a week ago she had declared herself, but after my initial worry, I had cast the idea aside. I had thought it a crush. When I had fallen from Sheba, she had led the search and it was she who had found me. She teased me, and we never had a cross word, even when we first met and she was so strict as a riding mistress and called me le modèle, taunting me. But apart from that one kiss, there was nothing.

'I have never given her cause Sophie.'

'You are naïve Trudi. A princess should know, that one does not have to do anything. Some people just love other people, they can't help themselves.'

'I am so sorry. This is terrible. Poor Wally, oh yes and poor Sabine too. What can I do?'

'Nothing, unless you love Sabine, in which case she will give Wally up. But I do not think you have to do anything Trudi. Just let it resolve itself. It will you know. I think already Wally knows that things are not right. See what happens on this trip.'

I tried to talk of other things as we made our way back to the villa. It was good to have Laurent there. He had a twin in each hand while Sophie and I swung Sébastien between us. We progressed slowly with three giggling, inquisitive, happy children. I could not have loved them more had they been my babies. To feel their vibrant hot little bodies in my arms, filled me with emotion.

I thought about Wally and Sabine. If anyone was an adult, then it was both of them. They were sensible adults, not given to rash decisions, tantrums or displays of emotion. I would have to do nothing and let them sort it out, but their marriage? Surely that would not happen.

Chapter 9.

We all met up at the Gare du Nord in the morning. It was now a large party, Nicole, Wally and Sabine, Thomas and Jacques, George Thibeau from Clermont and me. We emerged at Euston to find photographers waiting and we posed while they flashed away. Nicole was on the ball. She had given me an updated schedule on the train. I had a TV interview this lunchtime, followed by four more in the afternoon with magazines, then a dinner with the fashion press in the evening. Next day we were seeing two young bag makers and their work and dinner with buyers from the élite stores. Wednesday was a day off, I would see my family, Wally was going to his parents with Sabine. It would be a disaster. If Sabine did not love him, Wally would be hurt.

The rest of the party were just having a day in London. They had tickets for a matinee performance of 'Phantom'. I had two more interviews on Thursday before departing in the afternoon.

I was very nervous. I had asked Nicole to stick close to me. My previous times with the press had been more like clashes. The magazines were easy to handle, but live TV was different. They could just slip in that tricky question after the preliminary niceties and it could catch one off guard, particularly live.

I had decided to be open about my change and answer forthrightly if it was mentioned. After checking in at the hotel, Nicole and I left the others to go their separate ways and we headed for the TV studio. We were rushed through makeup and the green room, a short brief by the producer and we were on.

The questions were about Beauvonne and its rise in the fashion world, the tragic death of Simon and inevitably his accident and the death of Catherine too. Then it was me, my personal life and a little polite delve into my history. Was it an ambition to be a model and lead a fashion house? No, it had all happened by chance. I really still wanted to be a doctor and I hoped to revert to my studies next year. It all went well. I caught a sight of myself on the monitor and thankfully, I looked chic and attractive. I was pleased. Nicole said it had gone well.

In the afternoon we had a tight schedule of magazine interviews in my suite, but inevitably some overran their time. The Times planned a four page splurge for the Saturday magazine and Nicole thoughtfully provide some shots from past shows where I had modelled and they took a photo of me then with Nicole in the background.

A people magazine was quite probing about my sexuality. I found it quite annoying but answered matter of factly. They threw in a question about my relationship to Wally at the end. I was able to answer honestly, that we were at school together. We had been reunited by accident, I said, having lost touch after leaving school, but he was very good at his job. There was a lot more personal stuff about Simon's death and the children and being a Comtesse. The last I countered by saying that the title was not used and titles meant little in France. The woman commented on my French accent. I said I did not realise that I had one, but that I considered myself both English and French. At last they were gone. I was exhausted. We would be entertaining some of my interviewers again in the evening.

I had two hours to get myself ready for the evening. I had an hour's nap, then a shower and dressed. I wore a dark blue silk dress, V neck and three-quarter sleeves fitted with a pencil skirt. I wore no jewellery other than my wedding and engagement ring and diamond studs in my ears. I put my hair up but it was a mess. Nicole came to my rescue, twisting and pinning until it was neat tidy and attractive.

Nicole and I descended together in time to meet our guests as they arrived. They of course freeloaded on the champagne and cocktails, but the meal and service was exquisite. I was very pleased with the evening and pleased too, to get to bed just after one.

Tuesday and it was more relaxed. We were seeing two bag and shoe designers at their college. Wally was seeing his contacts while the rest of us went to see the young designers. Their work was impressive but as with so many students, the work while imaginative, much of it was quite impractical too. I left it to my designers and George to question them and to examine their work. Martine was a nice girl, very petite and quite dark. Her grandmother had come from Mauritius she said. Alexander Stevenson was Scottish, a tall boy built like a rugby player. After we had spoken to them I asked my people to make a decision. There was quite an argument. In the end they chose Martine.

'Are you quite sure?' I asked.

'Oui,' said George, 'I was playing devils advocate. We all agree. It is Justine.'

'Very well. Thank you gentlemen. You can go to wherever you want. I will now speak to her.'

I asked Nicole to fetch Martine.

She entered diffidently.

'We like you and your work Martine. I wonder whether you have thought about working in France, not knowing anyone. Can you do that?'

'I think so Madame Trudi. I have relatives from Mauritius there. I speak some French from my mother, but it is rusty and colloquial.'

'You will be working in Clermont Ferrand with George but also in Paris with the other designers. You will need to decide which of the two places to make your home. I would suggest that you stay with me in the Paris villa to start with, and you can decide later where is most practical. I am not always in Paris but there are others who live there most of the time.'

'Are you saying I have the job?'

'Oh yes, I'm sorry. If you are prepared to work in France, then we would like you to work for Beauvonne. Do you want to come to us?'

'Oh yes, thank you Madame, it is a dream come true. Really? I can't wait to tell my mum.'

'Good. So now you are working for us, you call me Trudi like everyone else. Are you free tonight?'

'Yes Trudi, I can be.'

'We are having dinner with the élite stores tonight. You know the ones I mean. I would like you to be there. So come to the Café Royal, the bottom of Regent Street at seven. Have you a frock?'

'Not a very good one.'

'Go to our shop on Bond Street and choose something, something chic. They will expect you and advise you. There is nothing to pay and you keep the dress. Make sure your shoes are right for the dress. Thank you for deciding to work for us. We expect great things from you. Say nothing to Alexander, just ask him to come in.'

'Thank you Trudi, thank you so much. I will not let you down.'

It was difficult telling Alexander, not that he made any fuss, but I felt sorry that we could not take him. He was a nice fellow and talented too, however my team had made the selection. He took it on the chin.

I took a taxi from the college and made for Knightsbridge. I wanted to see what two of the upmarket stores were offering. It had been a long time since I had strolled around a store. Simon had provided me with everything and I had been too busy for browsing. I tried to remember when I had last window-shopped and thought it was probably with Ellie. I thought about her and sex with her. She had been fun, but at the time I had been between sexes and totally vulnerable. We had not really kept in touch. I saw her at the wedding and I sometimes saw her on TV, reporting from some awful place in North Africa or the Middle East. She had aged and looked even more boyish.

I bought a Hermes scarf and some shoes, having browsed both stores and a couple of boutiques. I thought of taking the Underground to Piccadilly, just for the fun of it, but I was seduced by a passing taxi. In the hotel I had an hour before the hairdresser would appear to do my hair. I wallowed in a warm bath, emerging to moisturise and sort my things out for the evening. I was pleased when the hairdresser knocked the door. I had been alone for four hours and I was missing company. This was the time I would have been with Simon, an intimate time for us.

The hairdresser was quick and efficient, chattering all the time as they tend to do. I did my makeup, dressed and collected Nicole. We entered the bar just as the first of our guests arrived. I found Martine loitering uncertainly. I took her by the hand and put Jacques in charge of her. Wally was there to greet our guests and make introductions. Sabine, uninvolved in the Maison business had gone to a show, so we were a nice party of sixteen. It seemed a great success and the food was delicious. Wally, Nicole and I said goodnight to the last guest just after two. I put Martine in a taxi, asking her to be at the hotel for breakfast on Thursday.

I looked forward to a day off and a day with my parents.

A limo picked me up for the journey into Surrey. The tedious trek through the suburban jungle gave me a chance to review the last two days. Overall I thought the team had done a good job and I had made an impression even if it was only due to my history.

Most of the press had been fair, but of course two or three had to print my whole history as much as they knew of it, getting a lot wrong too. I particularly disliked one newspaper that constantly had a go at sexual minorities, and in particular transsexuals. The Mail seemed to think it had cut out a niche in the market for pseudo feminist trans-bashing. As I flicked through it, I came across an item of French news

'Paris Lawyer Arrested'.

A talented young lawyer was arrested last night for importuning as a female prostitute on the Champs Élysée. He was also charged with possession of a banned substance. He was named as Paul Morel.

I was shocked. I should not have been because I had wanted him in the gutter for the damage he had done and the money he had cost me. Franco and his connections had certainly done a thorough job. It was so unlikely that Paul would have cross-dressed and yet, after the way he had treated me, it was so apt too. 'Let the punishment fit the crime', W.S. Gilbert wrote for the opera 'Trial by Jury', I would have liked to see him as a prostitute. I wondered how they had contrived it. It was a terrible punishment and I suffered a twinge of regret, then I thought back. He had played with the future of my children and taken them from me and insulted me too, for personal gain. No, I said to myself, he deserved it. I imagined him sitting in a cell in torn tights and mini skirt and I laughed out loud. It would have been the most amusing sight, and he must have been most puzzled at what had befallen him.

We arrived at my parents' house, the first time I had been back for sometime. It all looked so plain and small, this 1930s built villa in its little avenue of almond trees. I was pleased to see that it had been freshly painted and the beach hedge was clipped and neat. I opened the gate and walked to the front door. I felt out of place in my expensive clothes. I felt a little sad too. So many memories wrapped up in that little house, of my confused and mixed up childhood. Mother must have been waiting in her bedroom overlooking the front garden, for the door opened as I approached. Mum and Dad stood waiting for me. I bent to kiss mother, and for the first time ever, she really hugged me to her and held me there and kissed my cheek. I felt embarrassed, wrong of me I know, but we were not, or used not to be that sort of demonstrative family. I wish we had been. It was not too late to change and I kissed them both.

To my surprise I found that Heather and her mother were in the living room. Heather rose as I entered and came forward to kiss me on both cheeks. 'You look lovely,' she whispered, 'my little sister Trudi.'

My mind went back to that awful afternoon when they had changed me from Timmy to Trudi, dressing me in Heather's hand me downs and sending us to the shops. How frightened and embarrassed I had been, hiding my face and wanting to cry, yet my spirit rising and rejoicing that I was at last being what I wanted to be.

'You'll do Trudi.' Heathers mother said. 'A real lady now, very grand. Yes you'll do.'

Heather seemed entranced by me, embarrassingly. We chatted together over the coffee and biscuits mother provided.

'Have you booked somewhere for lunch Father?'

'You brother has, but it is out at Cobham, The Old Plough. He says it is very good. I can drive.'

'No Father, I have the limo. We can all pile into that. If we are ready, we may as well go.' My phone whistled at me again. It had not stopped over the last fifteen minutes.

It was another ten minutes before mother had got herself in order and ready to meet the World. I touched up my lipstick.

In the limo, I put father in the front with the driver. I sat with Heather. I checked my noisy phone. I had ten emails to read and three voice messages. Three emails were about routine Beauvonne business. Two came from Martine, the first saying she would start in three weeks if that was alright? The second asked whether she should bring her car. I emailed back, yes to the first and to the second, sell it, she would have a company car.

There were two from Antoinette Dupois the lawyer. The first told me of Paul's arrest. The second sent two hours later stated that the police wished to speak to me.

I emailed back that I was shocked to hear of Paul's arrest. I said that I would be able to see the police on Friday and that I had been in England since Monday.

There was one from Nicole informing me that she and Thomas had split up. Could she look for a separate room? Oh dear, I was sorry, but in truth I thought it inevitable, they were so different and Nicole was so young, while Thomas was thirty three. 'Bien sür,' I replied with condolences.

Just as that text had gone I received another from Nicole. Thomas was returning alone after seeing his family, so Nicole would have the hotel room to herself. I hoped this falling out would not affect the running of Beauvonne.

My brother was waiting for us in the lounge bar when we arrived. There was a female officer sitting with him and they both rose as they saw us. I recognised Alison. They looked a handsome couple in their uniforms and I saw that he wore a crown on his epaulettes.

We kissed, more naturally than we had ever exchanged greetings. 'You are a major,' I said, 'congratulations. This calls for champagne. Can you drink or would that be wrong?'

'I think we can have a glass or two. You remember Alison?'

'Of course.'

We shook hands and I saw she had an engagement ring.

'Now brother, are you……?' I faltered, not wanting to put my foot in it.

'Yes Trudi,' Alison said, 'we are engaged.'

'Congratulations both of you. How wonderful. We must have champagne now.'

She was really pretty, even though without much makeup, prettier than I had remembered. Her blonde hair was caught back in a bun and I noticed she had captain's pips on her shoulders. Her hat lay upon the table. I longed to try it on, the whole uniform for that matter. Her hands were exquisite, long tapering fingers and nicely kept nails without polish. I liked the look of her, even more so than when they had come for Simon's funeral.

'When are you getting married?'

'In October, when we are both back from Afghanistan. It will be a last tour for us both.'

'And you are still in the army?' I asked.

'Medical Core, I'm in the regular army now, for three years.'

'Oh, so before, you were a Territorial. I've done five years medical study in Paris. I have taken a year off because Simon died and I have Beauvonne to look after, but I intend to start again next year.' We wandered together out of the French door that led onto a nice lawn, the sun warm on our backs.

'But how will you do that and manage the business?' she asked. 'And you are so chic and well presented in your lovely clothes. Won't a white coat and jeans feel so basic?'

'Until January, that's what I was like, well perhaps not jeans but ordinary store bought clothes and a white coat. I don't have to look like this all the time. Yes I do like to dress well, Simon taught me that it is good to make the best of oneself. I like fine things, materials that feel good on my skin and clothes that fit well, but if I know I can do that, I can also use a minimum of makeup and plain clothes. Are you judging me Alison?'

'I probably am Trudi. I have never met, as far as I know, a transsexual before you. I am sorry. My training did not cover it. Forgive my ignorance please. Tell me how it has been. Has it been hard?'

'Oui,' I had reverted to French, 'I mean yes, at times it was hard, hard being a boy, hating myself, my body and my clothes and perhaps most of all, other people treating me as a boy. You will not understand that, the subtle differences in treatment by parents, grownups, other children, according to sex. I changed permanently when I went into the sixth form. As a girl, teachers treated me in a completely different way to how it had been when I was a boy. And other pupils too, the ones that did not tease and try to bully. My life now is still a compromise. I am lucky, I look good, I lead a privileged life with money, but I am not perfect, and in some people's eyes, I will never be accepted as female.'

Alison looked directly into my eyes. 'Had I not been told, I would not have known. To me you are a very beautiful and sophisticated young woman, perfect and I have to confess, when I first saw you, I felt envious.'

'Of what?'

'Well, I am doing what I want to do, being a doctor and at the moment in the army, which needs people like me. But I saw you, the cover girl beautifully turned out and I let out a little gasp. Your brother had not prepared me for just how perfect you are.'

I felt myself blushing and my eyes watered. I turned away to look back at the hotel.

'I'm sorry. Have I upset you?' she asked.

'No. You are very frank. I think I am respected but few people actually express any sort of compliment like that. Simon did, he was continually boosting my confidence. But as we are being so frank, I looked at you and I was envious too. I thought I would love to wear your army cap and uniform and, you look lovely too. Blonde hair, lovely skin and good looks. I am glad my brother is going to marry you. I hope you will be my friend, my sister. I hope we will always be as close as we have been these few minutes.'

'I hope so too Trudi. Your brother is fond of you and even proud, but he did not say just how nice you are.'

'Not always nice.' I thought of Paul, the cloud hanging over me at the moment, with a visit to the police demanded on my return to France. 'And when we were children we hated each other.'

"I know, he told me. He is quite ashamed you know, of how he treated you.'

'I hardly understood myself, so why would a young boy have understood me? That is long passed. I am very proud of him now and we have made up. Come, we better go in and look at the menu.'

The meal was good. Mother managed not to tell any embarrassing tales of my childhood. It was a happy little gathering. Heather and her mother were quiet, I think overawed by us. Afterwards, we drank coffee and chatted in the deep leather armchairs of the lounge. When we parted I clasped Alison to me and I was nearly overwhelmed with emotion. I managed to control myself. My brother also kissed me. It meant so much, this tenderness that had really been absent from my family previously.

Back home, Heather and her mother went to their house. I had a cup of tea with my parents and then it was a tearful farewell from mother and even father controlled himself with difficulty. I suddenly realised that they really did love me, not just tolerate their deviant child.

It seemed a long journey back to London in the evening traffic. I needed to see Nicole and find out exactly what had gone wrong.

Chapter 10.

I knocked Nicole's door. It opened a fraction and I saw Nicole looking confused and embarrassed.

'Are you OK Nicole?' I asked. 'Can I come in?'

The door opened. I was surprised to see Wally and Sabine there, Wally sitting in an armchair and Sabine facing him perched on the bed.

'How are you all?' I asked. I realised it was a ridiculous question.

There was an embarrassed silence.

'We came to offer Nicole sympathy,' Sabine said.

'Of course, me too.'

'But I discovered something else, that she is in love with Wally.'

'Oh! Is that true Nicole?'

She was crying. She gave a nod, then sobbingly said, 'I am sorry, I cannot help it. As soon as he appeared, I was so entranced. I have tried to control it.'

'And that is why Thomas has gone home? He knew?'

'Yes Trudi, he guessed and I could no longer lie.'

'And you Sabine, how did you find out?'

'I overheard Nicole and Thomas arguing. I have confessed too, that I cannot marry Wally. He is wonderful, but not for me.'

I looked at Wally. 'Have you anything to say Wally?'

'Not at the moment.' He said.

'Is all this a shock to you?'

'I think you know Trudi, that things are not right between Sabine and me. I know you know that.'

'So what are you all going to do. You all work together. How was Thomas when he went home? I am very concerned that we do not lose him.'

Nicole had recovered some of her composure. 'He was OK. We weren't engaged. It just didn't work out. If you like I will resign Trudi.'

'And why on earth do you think that would help? I don't want these love affairs to interfere with the business of Beauvonne. You are so dear to me, and valuable. I need you all.'

'Thank you Trudi.'

'I need to know that you can all still work together, for Beauvonne, for all of us. Our futures are all bound together for our common benefit.'

'Well I can carry on,' Sabine said. "I do not love Wally enough to marry. I think you know that. I told you how I felt Trudi.'

'Sometimes, I like to ignore difficult things, and you were the girl friend of my best friend, Wally. I had hoped that my two best friends would marry, but it is obviously not to be. That is why I chose to ignore you. Perhaps I shouldn't have and all this would have happened sooner.'

There was a silence again. 'I suggest that we change and go down to dinner. We will have a civilised meal and talk. We all have to be honest with each other. Dinner in thirty minutes, and you will all be there. Don't let me down, or I shall be very annoyed.'

I left the room, a sudden chatter of voices starting up as I closed the door. I went down to the dining room and asked for a private room. They said that none was available but they could lay one up in my suite. I said that would do. I chose the menu, a set menu of crab starter, thick rump steak rare, and a trolley of sweets. I chose the wines, champagne, a wonderful rich chateau bottled claret, Ribena for adults and plenty of coffee for afterwards. I phoned Nicole for her to organise the rest.

I just touched up my makeup, changed my dress and then arranged the seating. I sat Nicole opposite me, Wally on my left and Sabine on my right.

When we were all seated, I asked Wally what he had achieved over the last three days.

'Both the Knightsbridge stores will have a Beauvonne section. I persuaded them to have a male and female shop in one place, separated by a wall with an arch and each would be labelled according to sex. It was not decided whether it would be in English or French. I thought to see what you thought?'

'What do you suggest Wally?'

'Given that the British are so incredibly ignorant over language, I first thought gentlemen and ladies. However, Beauvonne is French, enough rich people know that it is monsieur et madame. That is my suggestion.'

' I agree. And what about Edinburgh and Glasgow?'

'Edinburgh were undecided, they will let us know. But Glasgow is another story. They want a shop within a shop as soon as possible. Manchester are keen and Birmingham also. I will get designers on the layouts as soon as we are back in Paris.'

'Good Wally, thank you. Nicole, how has your courting of the British press gone?'

'Very well Trudi. The Times want to do a 6 pager on you now. Two fashion magazines something similar. OK want to do a 12 page centre fold, pull out of your whole life if you are agreeable. They are all coming in force to the next show. I have made quite a few connections with them and with some of the trade magazines and TV. A TV company wants to cover the next show, the planning, the models and makeup and dressing and the show, a look behind the scenes, so it is all very positive.'

'Excellent. Follow through with letters and confirmations when we are home won't you.

'Well I have news too. My brother is engaged to a lovely army doctor. I have never seen him so happy and settled. They are both off to Afghanistan for six months and plan to marry when they return. Oh and he is now a Major. It was lovely seeing my family. However, seeing Alison, my brother's fiancée, has reminded me that next year I shall be back learning to be a doctor. I need you all to be steadfast and diligent. I shall still be MD, but I expect you to make decisions. I have decided that I need an Assistant MD. I am appointing Wally as my stand in. Wally I want you to do what Simon did, that is see the six shops, Abu Dhabi, Shanghai, Beijing, Singapore, LA and New York. You will have to recruit someone for Europe, an assistant for you. And of course, you liaise with Nicole on marketing etc. Nicole will have to accompany you on some trips to arrange PR and marketing. I want to know that you can do that?'

'Sure Trudi, I'll not let you down.' Wally said quickly. 'Thanks for trusting me.'

'Nicole? If this is difficult for you emotionally, then I will have to find another role for you.'

'No Trudi, I will be fine.' I saw an exchange of looks between her and Wally.

'If you are both certain, then that is perfect. Now I have a confession to make. I have always loved Wally. At school when I was a boy, he was someone to rely on. When I became a girl he was like a big brother, protecting me as far as possible from the petty bullying and name calling. When we became heads of school, it was like we were a couple.' Wally was looking at me with a confused smirk. 'When I saw Wally's name on the list of applicants for salesman, my heart skipped a beat and when he appeared for interview, I had to use all my self control to be cool and business like. That is why I am making him Assistant MD. He is someone I love and trust. He is a man of good judgement.

'Nicole, you came to me in mid winter, in a shabby coat, fresh from feeding chickens. I liked you from the start. You have proved your worth, far and above anything I could have dreamt of and I love you like a sister. I could not run this company without you. So don't let me down please. You are very young, oh yes and I am 25, no age either, but be careful. You are very precious to me.'

Sabine sat with an amused expression. "And me Madame la Comtesse? What have you to say to me?'

'You Sabine, you are a tease. Madame la Comtesse, you know that annoys me, or le modéle. If you were not good at your job, I would sack you. But I need you too. I will not marry again. There cannot be another Simon, not even Wally could be that. I have three children to bring up. I must finish my studies and run Beauvonne. I too need someone to talk to intimately and Sabine has been that person. I believe in spite of her mockery, that she does love me. We will see. I hope now, all is well in the house of Beauvonne. Are we all happy?'

'Oui Trudi,' they chorused.

'We are a very young team. We can do this. What did the Three Musketeers say? All for one and one for all. A toast. To us and Beauvonne.'

'And to Trudi, my little sister, who waives her little wand and makes things happen.' Wally said.

'Trudi,' they repeated.

'I also know tragedy Wally, do I not? I am not feeling sorry for myself, but I nursed Simon through two terrible events and then he died. Anyway, just like my horrible school days, that is all behind us. I have enough to think about without wailing about the past. The future is what counts.'

Martine appeared for breakfast as I had asked her to. I gave her a cheque for her expenses for moving to France and a pack of ticket and map of how to find Maison Beauvonne and the Villa. She had already been designing she said. I asked her to do some research, find out where premium quality bags were made and to look at what the opposition were offering. Clermont Ferrand would have to be competitive to an extent with the Far East. Some manufacturers had a continuity of design from one bag to another, could she think about that? Inclusion of a motif around the B of Beauvonne would be good.

She made notes on her phone as I spoke. I liked that. I let her go and we four departed for Euston and our train.

The journey home was uneventful. The children rushed to hug me when I arrived at the villa, and Tasha dashed and leapt about. I changed into trousers and we all had supper. Then it was baths and bedtime for the children.

Nicole appeared later when I was sorting out my clothes and unpacking.

'Are you OK Nicole?'

'I think so Trudi. Wally and I went to the office to do some paperwork as you asked and then we went to a bar for a drink. I think he likes me at least. He has asked me to go to the cinema with him, a film he wants to see, a boys' film, but maybe I will like it too. Trudi it is a start isn't it? He kissed me on the lips when we said goodbye tonight, not a long lingering kiss, not a lovers kiss, but more than just friends or colleagues. I do so love him.'

'Why would he not love you? Actually, I don't think he really know what he wants. Was he ever really in love with Sabine? And then there was his Spanish girl friend. He seemed to give her up very easily. Nicole, I wish you luck with Wally, I love him too, but he is sometimes like a great ox, devoid of emotion.

'Now Nicole, business. Tomorrow I have to see the police about Paul. Apparently he has accused me of something. I want you to come with me to see Monsieur Barre. I am meeting Antoinette Dupois the lawyer at the Commissariat at ten. When that is done, can you go to the office and confirm in writing to Martine Kay? You have all the paperwork, so get her French papers too. Then over the next three weeks would you also organise a room for her here? Madame Gameau will sort it out, but I want you to make sure it is adequate. Also she needs office space, what are we going to do about that?'

'Trudi, there is a shop empty next to Maison Beauvonne. We could rent that or buy it if we have to, and knock through.'

'Excellent. Will you get things moving on that too. Now, on the way home it occurred to me that we are lacking. What don't we do?'

'I thought we had covered everything now Trudi. Bags are the last piece of the jigsaw.'

'Cosmetics Nicole. We have two perfumes, but a full range of cosmetics, lipsticks, eye shadows, mascara, foundation and the rest. I know you have a lot to do, but will you get on to that too? Oh and Nicole, is there anything you want, that you need for work. Is your car adequate, your computer?'

'Everything is fine. I am on top of it all Trudi. I would say if I could not manage.'

'I am going to give bonuses Nicole, and you will be rewarded. One last thing, what am I going to do about Sabine and her crush on me?'

'That is something beyond me Trudi, but I can assure you that it is not a crush. I have known for a long time that she is smitten. When you are in the same room her eyes follow your every move. I cannot advise you.'

'Oh dear. I do not want this complication. I still miss Simon. I know people take a lover to forget a lover but …..

'Is that the only objection?'

'What do you mean?'

'That you are two women. That makes no difference to me, but I like men. Do you want a lesbian relationship.'

'Ah, I see. I had a lesbian lover before Simon. He knew and he did not object, but when things became serious between us, I finished it. You may remember Ellie, the news reporter? I never loved her, more tolerated her. I do not know about Sabine, I mean I have never thought of her in that way, and I always leave the overtures to the other person. I will let you into a secret, and it is just between the two of us Nicole. I love men and women. I probably love women more because they treat me better. Would it shock people if Sabine was my lover?' I began to blush.

'In the fashion trade? You should know that anything goes these days.'

'I do not worry about my family Nicole but Sabine's father. He has always been suspicious of me. The semi feud between the two cousins was bad before I involved Sabine with the Beauvonne estate. It is good now, and your sister is serious with Laurent. It all seems rather incestuous doesn't it?'

'Non Trudi. You are not related to Sabine at all. You have given Sabine no reason to love you except, you are who you are. It is how you perceive her? Do you love her?'

'Yes, I do, but as a lover or a partner. Who knows.'

'Trudi, only you can decide, and whatever you decide, you have my support. I will always admire you and thank you for having faith in me.'

'Thanks Nicole. I think I will go to bed now if you don't mind, I am rather tired. I'll see you in the morning. Sleep well, and dreams of Wally perhaps.'

'Now who is the tease. Merci chère Trudi. Bon nuit.'

'Bon nuit chère Nicole.'

Chapter 11.

Monsieur Barre was pleasant. I was surprised to find him so polite because I had blamed him for Simon's death and threatened to prosecute him six months ago. This meeting brought back the pain I had felt then.

'Forgive me Madam, but an accusation has been made and I have a duty to investigate.'

'Of course Monsieur Barre, but I have no idea what accusation. Surely if I have committed a traffic violation, they will just send me a fine?'

'Madame it is much more serious. I will explain. I believe you employed a lawyer named Paul Morel.'

'Oui Monsieur, but no longer. I paid him for his services and dismissed him.'

'Why was that Madame?'

'You know lawyers Monsieur. Sometimes they will not follow instructions or are tardy. He was at fault in both categories.'

'So you fell out?'

'Oh yes. I was very upset with him because he had failed to carry out my husbands wishes that I would be the children's lawful guardian, at least it took him a long time to act and he charged me a great deal of money.'

'Are you aware that we have arrested him for importuning?'

'Oui, I read the papers. I was in London this week and read it in one of the British newspapers. I could not believe it. Surely there is a mistake?'

'Non Madame. It has been widely reported, so I may tell you the facts. At three in the morning of 26th May this year, Paul Morel was found dressed as a female on the Champs Elysée accosting men. A complaint was made by an Italian tourist, Vito Messana. The gendarme arrested Morel. He had traces of cocaine in his blood and was very inebriated. We examined his apartment and in spite of his protestations that he did not live a double life, we found a selection of female outfits, wigs and makeup in his wardrobe.'

'So Monsieur Barre, I have just returned from Londres yesterday where I have been since the 26th. What have I to do with this?'

'Morel maintains that you have had him framed as an act of revenge.'

'That is totally absurd monsieur. I freely admit that we had a severe disagreement. He was unprofessional, he saw an unprotected widow when Simon unfortunately died as you know Monsieur, and he thought he could take advantage. I paid him off and he and I parted. That was all.'

'He is of course now ruined Madame.'

'He should have stayed with the firm, Madame Antoinette's firm and all would have been well because they would have kept him in order. I have nothing to do with his other life. It is very sordid. I am broadminded Monsieur Barre, but if I think about Paul Morel after this, I will feel disgust.'

'Disgust is a strong emotion Madame. Why?'

'Because Morel did take me out on a few occasions, even kissed me when I was so sad and lonely. He was I found, merely grooming me, to fleece me, a common ploy of the worst kind of solicitor, and he stole a painting, one of my husband's favourites from the Chateau.'

'He returned the painting?'

'Yes.'

'You paid him off?'

'Oui Monsieur, €15,000. I gave him a cheque. That was the last time I saw him.'

'We know of that cheque Madame. It is a puzzle why he should blame you for his predicament.'

'Monsieur Barre, you have felt the heat of my tongue. You know that I can be let's say, harsh when I am shocked or hurt. I am sorry afterwards, as I demonstrated with you Monsieur when I blamed you for my husband's death. I want to be completely honest with you Monsieur and mention things I never talk about, my origins which are so painful. Sometimes, as a defence, I am rather harsh. It is a fault, but then given my origins, I have had to fight for acceptance. Paul Morel, yes we had a severe disagreement. He insulted me on the very matter I hate to speak of. He like you Monsieur was in the wrong, but with me, when something is over it is over.'

Barre was silent, a small smile playing about his eyes only. 'Oui Madame. Very well, I think that is all. Just be careful Madame with your temper, it could be it will get you into trouble one day.'

'Thank you for your good advice. Is that all?'

'Oh just one thing more. Do you know Monsieur Franco the restaurateur?'

'Oui . Nicole and I have been there several times. He likes the ladies, doesn't he Nicole? Why do you ask?'

'Oh just that your name came up when we were speaking to him.'

'He was very kind to me when Simon had his accident, when he lost his leg and nearly died and again when he had the first heart attack. The restaurant is near my Paris home, so when I am in trouble, I go there for what we term comfort food in England. Franco and his wife are very charming and simpatico. Why do you ask.'

'He mentioned that you were an occasional customer when we interviewed him on another matter. He thinks highly of you Madame.'

'It is reciprocated Monsieur. He is like so many Italians, charming to ladies, but also a sweet kind man. I am pleased to call him a friend and he me, I hope.'

'I see. Bien. Au revoir Madame Trudi. Thank you for your time.'

Nicole and I said goodbye to Antoinette on the pavement. I don't know what she thought. We then made our way to the Maison. Nicole drove.

As we waited at the traffic lights Nicole said, 'You are a smooth customer Trudi. I did not realise until now. You handled Barre excellently but he knows that there is much you are not saying.'

'I think you have a vivid imagination Nicole. Paul was a worm but I had nothing to do with his other life. To think he kissed me. It is disgusting.'

She took her hand from the steering wheel and placed it on my thigh momentarily. 'I don't ask questions of you do I Trudi. I do my job, but working for you is a pleasure, exciting and rewarding. I am here for you, you know that.'

'Thank you Nicole. I love you like a sister. You are a wonderful support. We have much to do today, and we are now late. I am going home tonight, to the Chateau. What are you doing?'

'I will stay in Paris, if you don't mind.'

'And Wally?'

'Oh he may meet me for a drink. We have duel visits to make plans for.'

'Of course Nicole. Go slowly, I do not want to see you hurt.'

'Wally will not hurt me, of that I am sure.'

'Nicole, regarding the cosmetics. Little Jean Rosier, who was researching stockings and tights. Get him to help you on cosmetics. If it works out, we will make him your assistant. Is that all right with you?'

'A good idea Trudi. He is a bright boy beneath his shyness.'

'You will know how to handle him and give him confidence. We need to encourage these youngsters.'

The rest of the day I worked hard tying up all the loose ends and preparing for Martine's arrival. I looked at the shop next door. For the present we could just take the upper floors and leave a lock up below or thinking of the future, take the whole thing. I decided that we would rent the whole building and the upper two floors would form the new design suite and the shop, which is thirty by ten metres, would make a showroom and selling area for cosmetics and bags. I left work at 6.30. Sophie and the children had departed in the afternoon and I took the Mercedes 4X4. I decided that I would change it, it was too large and a French fashion company ought to have French cars. I would speak to Peugeot. A 5008 would be more economical and take the children and Tasha. Maybe, I could do a deal with Peugeot. We could use each other in adverts. I was pleased with that thought. I phoned Nicole to make a note. Her phone was off so I left a message. By moving to Peugeot from Simon's beloved Mercedes, we would halve our car costs, with no loss of reliability. The only loss would be a little snob value.

It was after ten when I reached home. Everyone was in bed. I dropped my briefcase in the study and I too was soon in bed. When I awoke it was after eight. Today would be a day of relaxation for me. I decided that I would take Monday and Tuesday off, working from the Chateau. The rest of the week was free of appointments too so I would see if I could spend the whole week with the children.

By the time I was showered and dressed for riding, I could hear the children from below, and as I descended the stairs heard Sophie shushing them, saying they would wake mummy. I nearly sobbed when I heard that. Maman. I did not see enough of them but what else could I do. Life seemed to be a whirl. As I entered the salon there was a stampede to grab hold of me and I soon had the three of them clinging and asking to be lifted. I knelt and commanded a group hug. I said that I was going to ride with Sabine. In the afternoon, we would take their ponies out if they ate a good lunch.

Releasing myself from them, I went to find Sabine. I found her already in the stables grooming our horses.

'I hope you have not forgotten how to tack up,' she said. 'It seems a long time since we rode together. Do I have to do it or can you manage. I don't want you breaking a nail or something!'

'Still teasing Sabine. How do you expect me to love you if you are so disrespectful.'

'Love, have I asked for love? What is love, is it lust or is it a kind of fascination, an obsession. Do you know what love is Trudi?'

'Oui, je sais qu'est l'amour. I was in love with Simon, I loved the man not necessarily the manliness, but at times that too. You sound like that song by 'Foreigner,' a sad losers song, 'Do you know what love is?'

'You have an acid tongue today cocotte. Perhaps you will be in a better temper after a gallop. I will have a wager with you. If I win, and you have the faster mount, then you have a forfeit to pay.'

'And what is that forfeit?'

'I will decide after I see how you ride. Are you ready or do you need me to check.'

'I would like you to check Sabine please. I am never sure how tight the girth should be or the length of the stirrups.'

'You mustn't be frightened of tightening the girth. Tighten and then go back to it. They sometimes anticipate the girth and puff out their chests. Leave it and then go back and take it in again, taking them by surprise. I would have thought the marks on your saddle stirrups would tell you where they should be. No one else uses your saddle. Helpless woman!'

'I just like to have a servant.'

'Do it yourself then. I am no servant.'

'Please Sabine, I was teasing.'

'Do not tease me in that way. You know how I feel about you, but I will not be your dogsbody, your maid of all work. Do not take advantage.'

'I remember when we first met Sabine. You were so horrible to me.'

'Yes I was. Then I thought you a bit of a whore, I did not understand you or what you were. Now, I know you and I admire you. I have to thank you for turning my life around here. I was just a groom and you made me your estate manager. I love you, but you do not own me.'

'I love you as a person too Sabine, whatever our other relationship.' I mounted Sheba, turned and headed out not waiting for her. There was a clatter of hooves behind me and soon Sabine and her mount were alongside as we headed down the track towards the forest.

'Be careful Trudi. You have not ridden much this year, and sit up too. Shame on you.'

We trotted and then cantered a short way. The day was fine and warm and a large bumble bee droned past my head. The heat of the sun promoted the scent of the pines. When we moved through an area of more open land covered in gorse, the sweet scent was very strong, almost vanilla. It seemed that I had forgotten much for Sabine kept nagging at me, my feet my hands my seat, all were lacking in expertise.

After nearly an hour we turned down a drive that I had not been down before. 'Where are we now Sabine?'

'On my father's land. We are coming to a place where we can gallop.'

Soon after she sidled up to a gate and opened it. It led into a large field of open grassland. We both moved through and while I held her horse, she went back to close the gate.

When she was remounted she said, 'Here is where we race. I will give you two lengths start, but remember we have to stop before we reach the other side. When we pass that trough over there, that is the finish line. Loser pays a forfeit. You agree?'

'Of course. Just say when. My little Sheba will beat you on that old nag.'

'A half thoroughbred. Two lengths, yes that will do. You count to three and we go.'

I counted and dug in my heals. Sheba shot forward, I kicked again and we launched into the fastest gallop I had ever experienced. Sheba seemed to be eating up the distance and we were soon only a hundred metres from the finish. Sabine and her mount came charging by and she won by a head. I was disappointed.

'You knew you would win on that great big animal.'

'Of course, and I am a better rider, but you did well.'

'So what is my forfeit?'

'I am thinking about it. I will let you know.'

'More pay?'

'Don't be ridiculous.'

'Tell me. I hate being under someone else's power.'

'Like that bastard Paul. You sorted him out then Trudi. I will have to be careful. I do not want to be found on the Champs myself.'

'I don't know what you mean. Anyway, I would never do anything like that to you. So have you thought yet?'

'I know what I will ask you to do, but I am not telling you yet.'

'You are teasing me again Sabine, you are a bully. Where are we heading?'

'Back to Beauvonne and the forest. Don't worry. I will not hurt you.'

'I know you won't. It is just apprehension.' I found that I was excited by being in her power. I could feel a dampening in my knickers and my chest had tightened. I wanted to giggle like a silly young girl.

We rode in silence for a time, entering the forest again, insects buzzing in the still air. We came to the stream that fed the new lake.

'Let's stop here. Give me your reigns and I will tether them to this tree.'

I waited for her next move. I felt strangely vulnerable.

She took my hand and guided me to a large fallen tree. I brushed at it with a gloved hand before I sat and she laughed.

'You are such a girl Trudi.'

'So what is happening Sabine. Have I to undress and race through the forest naked or ride topless? What evil plan have you dreamt up.'

'I want a kiss. Just one kiss. That is not such an ordeal is it?'

'No, we are always kissing.'

Our mouths met and of course it was not our usual friendly kissing. I melted into her firm embrace and accepted her roving lips that made my face tingle, and an involuntary moan escaped as my senses yielded to her. She released me, looking deeply into my face as if searching for a sign.

'Sabine. Such an elaborate plan for that small favour.'

'Not a small thing for me Trudi. Something I have dreamed of for three years.'

'But before Wally, had you had girl friends?'

'You mean lesbian lovers?'

'If you like.'

'A girl at college, a crush. I thought it of no importance, although it was painful at the time. It was unrequited as my love for you has been. First you were Simon's bit on the side, son putain, then his wife and then you engineered my liaison with Wally. All that time I was attracted to you, but because you were unattainable, I left you alone. I had fantasies, wet dreams about you. It was only as Wally and I became intimate that I thought more and more of you. Wally was very kind, but he knew. He asked and I told him. When we made love, I pretended it was you, but it did not work. I loved Wally, that big clever ox, but it was not right for me.'

'You know Sabine, that I have had a lesbian affair, my friend Ellie. Yes, oh I told you didn't I? Oh well it was a long time ago, and I ended it because I fell in love with Simon who was so good to me too. And with Ellie, I was very inhibited. I was so shy about my body, my change. She loved me before and after my operation, It was all very puzzling. I hated my male body yet she in some ways seemed to like a boy with breasts. Outwardly I was cool, inside I was quaking about her demands. I was just her toy. I tried to remain remote as I have been with you too. Poor Sabine.'

'Yes and all the time you were such a little cocotte (darling), in your girlie clothes and on television. I used to dream of you constantly, holding my breathe when you appeared.'

'Cocotte not coquette at least that is something to be proud of. Do you not dream of me still?'

'Et tu Trudi. Who do you dream of?'

'I don't. I take a sleeping pill, well half of one, and I do not dream. Too many nightmares in my life, real ones Sabine.'

'Ah ma pauvre. There, one never knows what nightmares another suffers. Oui, I can understand. It is enough that you have suffered so with Catherine and then Simon, but your early life was difficult, yes?'

'Not easy Sabine. However, I think I remain reasonably sane. So what do you want from me?'

'I would like to live with you, as your partner, but I do not know how you feel about that. You must be honest with me.'

'And what would your family say about that?'

'They don't have to know. I would say you are lonely and asked if I would live in. Perhaps one day, I would tell them. Maman would understand, I think she knows anyway.'

'But your Papa, he is suspicious of me anyway. What would he say?'

'That is why I will not tell him immediately.'

'I cannot give you children Sabine. What is more, I don't really approve of gay parents. I'm now guardian, maman to three children. They are my first responsibility. If you had children too, it could be a complication.'

'I do not need children. I know some women would cut off an arm to be pregnant, but I have yet to feel that urge. One never knows about the future.'

'Why don't we give it a try then. I may annoy you Sabine, or you me. But I have no hang ups about sleeping with a woman. But I do want it to be discreet at the moment. So no hints, no telling a best friend or your brother. You can have Simon's old room and there is a connecting door to mine. So we keep up the pretence for the time being.'

'Even from Sophie?'

'Oh yes, from Sophie and Nicole. If one of them should know, then Laurent would know, and then your mother and later your father. Why upset them if it is not going to work out. Your crush on me may not last.'

'You think after three years it is just a crush? Do you not like me at all?'

'Yes I love you Sabine. But can I stand living with you? Let us have this trial marriage, then we see.'

'This has gone better than I had hoped. Can I stay tonight?'

'Yes Sabine. Do you need to get things from home?'

'Oui. I shall tell maman that you are distraught after being interviewed by the police. Oui, Sophie told me everything.'

'Oh! Well then. Tonight's the night Josephine.'

'What?'

'In England we have a saying, about Napoleon and Joséphine. We say not tonight, Joséphine when Napoleon is too tired. It is like a joke.'

'You Anglais. Mad people.'

'Yet you love me, and you know, I am now French too. I am une Franglaise.'

'Oui, and a mad person.'

Chapter 12.

Sophie and I spent the afternoon with the children. We drove to Lisieux where there was a good children's playground, swings, slides, a zip wire and a roundabout. The family slide was wide enough for three, so I climbed up with the children, with one twin on each side and Sébastien on my knees, we whizzed down. They giggled, André doubling up and falling over. 'Again'.

We did it three times, After that, I shepherded them up the ladder and I sent the three of them down together holding hands. To my relief they emerged unscathed. They tried all the other slides, then the swings and lastly the roundabout. I thought they would never tire, but finally they consented to go to a café for their tea. They all fell asleep on the way home and we carried them indoors.

We quickly put them to bed. Cook was off so I went to the kitchen. I cooked some packet breaded fish, potatoes and two vegetables. Sabine entered the kitchen just in time for me to do her some as well.

As we three ate, I said casually to Sophie, 'By the way Sophie, Sabine will be staying in the Chateau for the time being. She will use Simon's room for now.'

'Good Trudi, she will be company for you too, n'est ce pas?'

'She is almost my oldest friend in France, Sophie, so yes, it will be good to have a companion again.'

'Laurent said he thought this might happen, some time ago.'

'Did he now? He must be a fortuneteller. Anyway, it ought to give you more time off at weekends Sophie, because there will be two of us to look after the children all the time, and in the week, if I am in Paris, you will have company. It should suit everybody.'

'I think it is a good solution Trudi.'

'Sabine you are very quiet, have you changed your mind.'

'Not at all, I was just listening to you two chattering girls. So what does Laurent think Sophie?'

'Laurent? He thinks like I do, that Trudi needs companionship and as you both like each other, it is a good solution. Your mother too.'

'Oh! You have all been talking. So quickly. I only said to Maman that I was moving to the Chateau at lunchtime, yet you have all had time to discuss it. Fantastique. Et mon père? Perhaps you have also heard his opinion.'

Sophie shrugged and smiled.

'What did he say Sophie?' I asked.

'I just told you.' She shrugged again. 'That's it, all he said. A shrug. Your mother asked him what he thought and that was his only reply.'

'So much for our privacy,' I said. 'Oh well, perhaps it is better. But Sophie, we are not making a public announcement, so we keep it in the family.'

'Then I think you should speak to Nicole. I think she knows, but it would be better if you confided and of course, Wally too.'

'You are right Sophie. There cannot be a secret in my family, as I think of you all. But the rest, well they can surmise but that is as far as I go. To the World I am a lonely and tragic widow.'

'And you have been Trudi. Your 'family' all know what you have endured. It is time you had some love again.'

'Bless you Sophie. What on earth would I have done without you and your sister?'

'There is something you can do for me.'

'Anything?'

'Laurent stays over sometimes. I let him in and out, using the back stairs and the rear entrance. I would like him not to have to live like a thief.'

'That is little to ask. Of course, you know you have my blessing. You had better give him a key. Oh I need to give you one too Sabine. If you have eaten enough, perhaps you could load the machine. I am going to the study, one or two things I have to do. After that I am going to turn in. I am very tired. All these emotions have knocked me out. I'll say goodnight now.' I kissed them both.

In the study I wrote to the agent for the shop next to the Maison making an offer. Next I researched cosmetic manufacturers so that I would have enough background knowledge to make a decision.

I sent Wally an email asking him to help Nicole with the arrangements for visiting our main outlets.

I climbed wearily to my bedroom. I stripped while the bath ran. I looked at my posy in the great mirror before it steamed over and the memories flooded back. Simon's love was all so new then. It seemed an age ago. I was suddenly sad, yet I knew I had so much to be thankful for. My marriage to Simon had been for such a short time but it had been very happy. He had been a doting and spoiling husband, generous in the extreme, yet remained my master. In all that time we had no crosswords. He made decisions, like our honeymoon that was also a business trip, but I did not mind. Just being with him, being his, was enough. I had a life besides him and Beauvonne, learning to be a doctor, but the rest of the time I was his, to dress, to experiment with, to help him be the father he should have been. The rewards had been so many. He had been ill twice in that time, and I was there for him. I loved taking care of him.

I feel now that I should have saved him. If only I had pressed Barre, I may have recued him from the police cell and he could have lived. Now I was mistress of Beauvonne and I felt a terrible fraud, living this privileged life due to his death. He had been so young, not yet forty.

I washed myself and just lay relaxing, half asleep, listening to the various noises of the house, creaking boards as people moved about, water running, pipes expanding and contracting. I was mildly depressed, thinking about the past and the future without Simon. What would he have thought of Sabine moving in as my partner? I decided that if he were to be looking down on me from heaven, he would smile, but he would expect me to behave with decorum and look beautiful. The door pushed open and Tasha came in. She spread herself on the bath mat, her brown eyes swivelling slightly to see me. I closed my eyes.

I did not hear her come in. I roused myself to leave the bath and was aware that a towel was to hand. Sabine had spread the towel like a screen for me to cloak my body, her face turned from me to preserve my modesty. I drew it about my body and stepped from the bath as the water started to gurgle down the drain. I sat on the bathroom stool, my back to her. I took body lotion from the shelf and flipped it open.

'Sabine, would you cream my back for me please?'

'Of course.' She massaged my back. 'And the rest of you?'

'If you like Sabine, it would be nice, but I do not want you to feel like a servant.' I looked at her through lowered lashes out of the side of my eyes. I saw she was wearing quite girly pyjamas, an unembellished top in eau de nil and calf length pink trousers.

'I want to feel your body under my hands. Am I sleeping with you tonight?'

'Yes if you want to, but I do want to sleep. Can we just cuddle Sabine. I am so tired.'

'It is enough to be with you Trudi.'

Tasha eyed us, showing the whites of her large eyes. We entered my large bed, Tasha settling at the bottom, and I switched out the light. Sabine and I kissed good night, and she cuddled into my back, her arm passing over my waist and her hand upon my stomach. It was very comforting. I felt warm, loved and safe. I had not felt so contented for a long time. I fell asleep. I was aware of Sabine in the night as I turned, and realised that there was a sexual attraction caused by the body beside me but I dropped asleep again immediately. I awoke refreshed in the morning, Sabine's arm and leg across me still. I removed myself carefully and she merely repositioned herself in the bed.

It was still early. I heard some noise from the nursery and putting on my dressing gown, I went to see what was happening. The children were in boisterous mood, the twins chasing each other and Sébastien racing after them. Sophie appeared from her room.

'I am sorry Trudi, I was just saying goodbye to Laurent. It won't happen again.'

'No Sophie, it mustn't. I want you and Laurent to have a good time, but when the children are in your charge, you are working and they come first. No damage done, but it must not happen, please Sophie.'

'Non Trudi. It will not. Et tu, how are you this morning?'

'I had a good rest thank you, the best sleep for some time. I have so many awful thoughts in my head at the moment, of letting Simon down, of my brother and Alison going to Afghanistan and the worry of everything. That Paul

Morel did not help, he alone caused me nightmares. Then the business and all my family, it has been a strain. However, I have lost two kilos in weight and I am pleased. I hope Sabine will share some of the worries I have kept hidden for so long and help me think them through. She is still sleeping. May I say Sophie, thank you for being so supportive with Sabine living here. I do not know what will happen, but you were right, I need someone to love me and someone to love.'

'Ce n'est rien. You are good to us all Trudi, it really is like a family. We support each other, n'est ce pas?'

'Et tu? How was it with Laurent now he is not sneaking in and out?'

'It was good. And the children just think their uncle comes to stay, so do not worry about that.'

'Good, just remember that they are unpredictable and may barge in at the wrong time. I am sure we will work it all out Sophie. I'm going to get dressed, then we can dress these little ones and go down. Why don't you see what Laurent is doing and Sabine and I can look after them today?'

'He is going to horse racing, a small meeting but he knows everyone there. I'll phone him, thank you Trudi.'

At breakfast, Sabine announced that she had to move the sheep to new pasture, moving the electric fence to give them fresh grass. The children were excited to do it and we all set out for the far end of the parkland.

Sabine gave them each a job to do, carrying the fence posts one at a time, while I hammered them in and Sabine moved the wire. It took a long time, but it was good to see the children joining in with the work of the farm. Sabine's border collies kept the sheep in order until we were done.

We made a merry party, the children running over the pasture to the Chateau, and Sabine sending the dogs to round them up. She stowed the dogs in the stable and we washed up and changed our shoes. I decided that as it was Sunday we would eat out. I rang Rive Droite in Alençon. They were as usual accommodating. They could fit our little family in at two o'clock.

I decided that the children should look their best so we changed them. I put on a dress and tidied myself and found that Sabine too had made an effort. She wore smart slacks with a white feminine blouse. I was pleased. I did not particularly want a female partner who took no pride in her appearance. I suddenly found her very alluring. It was a curious feeling and I could not understand why I saw her in a different perspective. I brushed Tasha and we piled into Sabine's Land Rover.

As we left the car and walked over the bridge, the twins walked ahead, jumping from paving slab to paving slab, trying to avoid the cracks. I held Sébastien in my arms and I felt Sabines arm casually encircle my waist. It was very arousing and I blushed as I looked sideways at her. She appeared not to notice.

In the restaurant, the staff were very welcoming. I had been there only once since Simon died. The owner was very solicitous with kisses on both cheeks and held onto my hand. It was lovely, oh it was commercial too, the typical act of a restaurateur, but it was nice to have the attention and I think genuine sorrow. He showed us to a table in La Terrace, and a bottle of champagne arrived but I explained that we were driving and would have just one glass today. We all chose to have breaded sole to start, one portion shared by the children, with a little lollo rosso salad with a mustard mayonnaise, followed by roast lamb and grilled vegetables. I wished my mother had cooked it. It was her speciality and she did it well. We finished with fig and pomegranate flan with crème anglaise. The owner reappeared with an iced cake to take home for our tea, in lieu of the champagne we had refused.

Throughout the meal Sabine had been attentive to the children, helping cut their meat and making sure they had clean plates. Tasha at our feet was denied any titbits due to a stern non from Sabine. It allowed me to relax more. Even Simon had not been this attentive to the children, leaving behaviour to Sophie and me, while he told his stories.

Sabine drove us home and I rested my left hand upon her thigh and fell asleep until we rounded the gateway to Beauvonne.

We piled out, the children still full of life. Tasha saw Mitzi sitting on the top step and ran to see her and they chased indoors through our legs as soon as the heavy door was pushed open.

We played board games with the children until tea-time as the afternoon had become cool and wet. Sophie and Laurent came in at five.

Sophie made tea for us, toasted teacake, followed by the iced cake we had been given. With the children in bed, we watched TV, sitting as couples, feeling quite natural. It had been a wonderful day. I was more contented than I had been for the last six months. We were all tired and we went to bed early.

Chapter 13.

'So,' I said when we were both settled in bed, 'this girl you had a crush on at University, did you sleep with her.'

'Why do you want to know?'

'I just wondered how experienced you are in a lesbian relationship? Are you going to be fumbling about or do you know what to do?'

'She was experienced, I was an ingénue. Why do you want to know? Is it jealousy?'

'No, not jealousy, it would be absurd to be jealous of what happened before we met or before we became involved, but I would like to know that I am attractive in my own right, that I am not just a substitute for that first love.'

'Oh, you want me to boost your ego. I am not going to. I want to keep you guessing.'

'Do you? Aren't you interested in my relationship with Ellie?'

'You already told me that she pursued you, so I think your ego is boosted enough.'

'So then ingénue do you know what to do?'

'Oh yes Trudi, ma Princesse.' Her hand moved up my thigh and she bent over me and kissed me, her tongue moving around my lips and I was immediately aroused. Without thinking at all, I wrapped my leg around her and clasped her to me as her hand moved into my vulva and so gently up to my clit. I writhed with pleasure and excitement. Neither Simon nor Ellie had aroused me so quickly.

I moaned and Sabine moved between my thighs, linking her hands behind my back she raised me towards her, my back arched. She kissed both nipples and sucked my right nipple until I thought she would swallow me. She lowered me down, her hand worked on my clit and I thought I would burst. I came amazingly quickly. She laughed.

'You are just a little chicken. I was nervous that I could not please you after being a married woman. I am relieved.'

I moved a hand to her vulva but she moved away. 'No I do not want you to. Arousing you is enough for me. Now I know this is going to work. I love your body, it is so lithe, yet so feminine. Are all models like that?'

'No Sabine, they are all ugly. You do not want to chase after them, you would be disappointed.'

'I do not want anyone else.'

'Then tell me Sabine, and you never have. You have teased and insulted me, but never said you love me. Tell me.'

'I do not love you, I adore you.'

'Is that more than love?'

'It is twice as much, ma petite poulette.'

'A farm animal? Is that what I am mademoiselle agriculteur.'

'No, you are our little princess.'

'Then serve me again my Sabine, because the first time I thought I was dreaming.'

Afterwards we lay exhausted. She tasted my cum and declared it tasted sweet. We lay tightly together and I caressed her nape hair that seemed to have the same effect as stroking a cat. She almost purred. We fell asleep. When I awoke it was light and I was alone. Sabine must have gone to work I concluded. I lay thinking about our lovemaking. I had wondered whether this relationship would work, whether she could arouse me as Simon had. I realised that it was even better. I felt happier than I had in the last six months.

I ran a bath and soaked in expensive salts. I moisturised and dressed carefully in trousers and baby blue silk shirt, did my face and waved my hair.

At breakfast with the children and Sophie, she said. 'You look radiant this morning Trudi. I have never seen you so glowing. It is though a light has been switched on inside you.'

'Thank you Sophie and you too.'

'Oh, I am used to it, but it is agreeable with Sabine, yes? I can see such a change. I am pleased for you.'

'I feel better than I have for a very long time. I am going to ride Sophie. This afternoon, it is supposed to rain. I think as we shall be indoors, we should read to the children and teach *them* how to read.'

'Oh the twins can read a little already, but it is a good idea Trudi.'

After lunch we managed to settle the children down after a few games and a story. We started to read together. I found that Sophie was indeed correct, they could already read a few familiar words. With a twin on each side of me, we read Jack and the Beanstalk. I made the voice of the Ogre and Jack's mother and they were engrossed and attentive. Sébastien joined in as best he could, sitting on Sophie's knee behind me as we three sat on the floor. After the story we played counting with a bag of old francs Their counting to ten was good but after that they tended to make it up.

It was children's teatime when Sabine appeared. To my surprise she came straight to me and kissed me openly in front of Sophie who did not appear to notice. I was touched by this open affection and excited by the kiss.

I thought of Ellie, and how restrained I had been, frightened of acknowledging our liaison, shy and timid. With Sabine, it all felt so natural, even more so than with dear Simon. We all three put the children to bed.

Dinner followed. Afterwards we sat and talked, Laurent came in and we watched some TV. I was dying to know what Sabine's parents were saying, but did not like to ask.

Tuesday morning Nicole phoned reminding me that our accountant had started work. It had gone completely out of my mind. I found Sophie and told her I had to go to the office but I would be back in the evening.

I found Jeanette Cassar in her small office space peering into her computer, a huge pile of papers on one side of her.

'I am sorry Jeanette. I have been away in the country and my children needed my attention. Is there anything I can do for you?'

'No Madame Chartrand. I just have to get these accounts entered and then post all the invoices for the year to date. So from the beginning of this year, I should be able to tell you at anytime how the business is. I don't know how you have managed until now. It is just a muddle.'

'I am afraid that my husband was a gentleman, not a businessman. You know that he died in January, and I have been running Beauvonne since then. We are expanding the range, moving into bags, cosmetics and even stockings and tights. I am afraid that our own accountant was the last change that came to mind. However, I think I deserve credit for realising we needed you. Mademoiselle, now that you are here, how long before you can give me some meaningful reports. I want to know whether we are making money, how much and on what? Perhaps you will inform me when that is done?'

'Bien sûr Madame Chartrand.'

'Good, but you can call me Trudi, everyone else does, and you are Jeanette, n'est-ce pas?

'Oui Trudi. Merci.'

'So welcome to Beauvonne Jeanette. I hope you learn to like us here. We are a young team and expanding quickly. I expect you to keep us solvent. Nicole or Wally can always find me. There is I think a list of all phone numbers in your desk. Don't hesitate to phone if there is a problem.'

I found Nicole and Wally. I took them to lunch.

'I expect you know by now, the family grape vine seems so active, that Sabine has moved into the Chateau.'

'You are so coy Trudi. Moved into the Chateau? What are you really saying?' Wally asked.

In spite of myself, I blushed. 'Sabine and I are giving it a trial, seeing whether we can live with each other, as a couple. There, I have said it. I don't know why I found that so difficult, because you already know, but it is a big thing for me. She loves me and I think I love her, I suppose in a way, we always loved each other, but not sexually. Anyway. So what do you think?'

'I think it is wonderful for you both Trudi,' Nicole said, 'if Sabine can bring you joy and find herself, then it is wonderful. We all knew for months that she was in love with you. We were all just waiting for it to happen.'

'So why did you not part from Sabine Wally?'

'Because I liked her, liked her a lot. I realised that while she loved me, it was not a sexual thing. I hoped that something would change, but when Simon died, I really knew it was the end, if you gave Sabine the green light. In the meantime, I cried on Nicole's shoulder, poured my heart out to her, not wishing to trouble you. We grew closer and closer until it all blew up in London. Nicole was unhappy with Thomas.'

'I was not seriously unhappy, that is wrong, it was OK, but It was not heart stopping infatuation with Thomas, whereas I could hardly breathe when Wally was close to me.'

'Are you happy now Wally? You are not going to hurt Nicole?'

He looked at me with that half smile he had regarded me with so often. 'Have I hurt anybody? No, this is the real thing. I hate being apart from her. We can't bear to be apart. She is extraordinary as you know.'

'And Thomas, Nicole, how is he?'

She shrugged. 'I know you want one great happy family Trudi, you always have, but sometimes relationships do not work out. Thomas is OK. He is seeing one of the cutters, but he is not my responsibility is he?'

'No Nicole, you are right. I just don't want to lose him. You both have my blessing, that sounds patronising but I don't mean it to be. You don't know how fond of you both I am, and it could not be better, that two of the best people I know are together.'

'We go back a long way Trudi,' Wally said, 'I have seen the before and after. There was a time at school when I thought you completely bonkers and you would go right off the rails. That was before I knew the real you, the girl trying to escape from the boy. Then when we became head boy and girl, I found underneath the girly sweetness is a genius for planning and problem solving. I am a great admirer. I am pleased that I applied for the Beauvonne position. It has given me so much, including Nicole and working with you again. I hope that things work out for you and Sabine. I love you both and you both deserve happiness. Nicole and I will not let you down.'

'Oh I am confident of that Wally, I could not have two more able lieutenants. I am very happy with Sabine, but I am not coming out publicly, so it stays in the family, the inner family, you two, Sophie and Laurent, Sabine's family, oh yes they know already. But to the rest here, I am tragic Trudi, young widow. I do not want the press at my door again.'

'We haven't discussed it at all. We were waiting to see what happened.'

'OK. Is there anything else to discuss or can I go back to the Chateau and do some serious bonding.'

'You can leave it to us, but after the conference, we are off on tour, so perhaps you need to be here?'

'Bien sûr.' I said.

'Trudi. Bon chance with Sabine.' Nicole said. We all kissed and embraced.

I returned to the Chateau, to my children and my lover. This was perhaps the happiest week of my life. Sophie went into Alençon on Wednesday, leaving me with the children. I took them for a walk in the forest with a picnic, piggy-backing Sébastien when he tired. The twins had to count the animals they saw, and Sébastien shouted out when he saw one, holding onto my hair as if he was using reins. It was a gorgeous day of bright sunshine and I really felt like their mother, alone with them for the first time. At last we had really bonded, they threw them selves at me and pulled at me calling me Maman. Tears filled my eyes as realisation of this new relationship dawned. They asked why Maman was crying and I said that it was because I was so happy, which made the twins giggle.

We walked back via the stables to see the horses and ponies and found Sabine talking to her workers. I took the children up to bathe, dressed them in their PJs and down again for tea. Sabine came from washing herself and kissed me on the lips. The children appeared not to notice at all. Together we put them to bed, reading them a story and Sabine taught them a new song.

Sabine and I ate dinner alone. Afterwards we sat cuddled up watching "Before Sunset' a romantic movie. We went to bed before Sophie returned.

So the week went by, my life revolving around the children, working a little in the evening answering emails and planning. I decided to take the next week off too. My bonding with the children and Sabine, had gone well and I did not want that to slip. I asked the Maison management to come out to the Chateau the following weekend for Friday and Saturday nights. I wanted all the management to gather so they all knew what each other was doing and could coordinate. I also wanted updates on their current actions. I asked each of them to prepare a five minute status report for the conference. The list of managers was getting longer.

Martine Kay was arriving Friday and Nicole would bring her and little Jean Rosier who was looking at stockings and tights and helping with research into cosmetics. The designers, Thomas and Jacques, Wally, the cutting room staff, another four and the office manager and Jeanette were all coming. I had rooms, not all luxurious, and some would have to share, but they would do. We would have the meeting from nine Saturday morning until it finished. In the afternoon Sabine arranged for clay pigeon shooting and archery as a team builder. Afterwards people could walk the forest. For the evening I booked a room at Rive Droite and a coach to transport us all.

The next week went quickly too. Nicole reported in each day with an update on the arrangements she was making and helping the office manager with the show arrangements. It was only six weeks away. This year the shows would take place on Le Champ de Mars, with the backdrop being the Tour Eiffel. The tented area was centred on Rue Anatole France. She assured me that everything was in order, the site secured, the tent hired and booked, security staff and models booked and transport and catering arranged. This would be our biggest show ever. I would not be modelling as such, but of course would make an introduction and sign off with a little speech at the end. I was determined to be chic and dignified as befits the owner of a couturier salon.

Sabine was busy with the estate. It would soon be harvest and she had her own preparations in hand, harvesters booked and a list of backup contractors should one fail. We rode the estate on horseback, all one day, taking a packed lunch.

The estate had never looked better. The hedges were now long with summer growth and the headlands, left fallow for wildlife, were deep in grass and wild flowers Sabine had sown. The crops looked pristine, no wild oats poking up their shaggy heads and the ripening barley was just on the turn from green to gold. Potatoes and sugar beet looked healthy as did the beans and root crops. The estate roads were all in good condition, Jean Luc's father really was earning his keep. Sabine's lake, now two years old looked divine, natural and beautiful and I could see that the new avenue she had made of lime trees at tremendous cost, would be a great asset. Lastly we visited the sheep. They looked terrific, shorn, quietly grazing, moving out of the way of our mounts as we rode amongst them. We now had five hundred, and Sabine had ploughed up extra fallow land that Simon had neglected to manage, and it was over sown she said with special grass mixes clover and other legumes.

We rode back through the forest and came to the ford across the brook. We crossed and dismounted to eat the last of our food. I realised that I was already aroused, just sitting next to her on the grassy knoll. I put a hand on her thigh. She turned to me, her face serious. She took my head in both her hands and kissed me gently on the lips.

'So you do really like me, ma Comtesse?'

'Oui, je t'aime Sabine. I think I never loved anyone more. Don't ever leave me.'

'Then you don't wish to find another man to replace your beloved Simon?'

'No Sabine. I just want you. Thank you for being here for me. Sabine, when we have the show, I would like you to be there in Paris. I do not want to come out publicly, I do not feel strong enough, but I would just love to have you near me.'

'It is harvest time. We have to make a plan that can change according to what is happening here, and the weather is our master, but I promise that if I can be there, then I will be.'

'Thank you Sabine. I hope you will be able to come.'

'You are a funny girl.'

'Why? Do I annoy you?'

'No, Madame Trudi, you charm me. I know you are really strong but also so demure, almost submissive. You are such a little femme.'

'It is easy to submit to someone I love.'

'But you are also my boss. Never forget Trudi, that you are number one. I want you to love me, but you always should love yourself a little bit more. If you give yourself up completely to someone, then you bury your soul and that is not right.'

I was silent for a time, trying to work that out. 'To tell the truth Sabine, you are really my first love. Oh I loved Simon, but it was partly because he was a Godlike figure, he created me in a way and was so kind to me that I could not do otherwise than love him. But with you, it is different. I love you, well, because I do, because I am infinitely attracted.'

'Emotionally, you are very immature Trudi! I won't have you subjugating yourself to me. You are a wonderful person, very talented, more so than me. I am a good farmer but you are going to be a wonderful doctor as well as the head of Beauvonne. I could not do all you do. Just because I make you feel something in your poor deprived heart, does not mean that you should give yourself up completely. If you do that, then I would not respect you. Simon told me after he came back with just one leg, how you sat with him everyday for sixteen hours a day. Then there was all that business with Paul Morel. You were so strong. You must stay strong. Come, we are getting too serious. I will race you to the end of the forest. No cheating!

We mounted and after a count of three we were into a gallop, hoofs thundering, my knees gripping tightly to the saddle. She was alongside, then slightly behind, and somehow caught up again. I dug my heels into Sheba once again and she pulled ahead just as we reached the end of the forest.

We stabled our horses and groomed them, filled their water and gave them their feed. Outside the stables I danced around Sabine. 'I beat you slow coach, I beat you, I beat you.'

'Is that how a Comtesse should behave?' she asked, tossing her head.

'It is the way your lover behaves. Loser.'

Her hand was about my waist as we entered the rear door to the Chateau, and she pulled me hard to her and kissed me quite savagely. 'That is my Trudi. That is why I love you.'

'I don't know why I love you, I just do. I think I always have, even when we first met and you were so hard. You thought me a putain! Oh well, I suppose I was in a way, Simon coming to me more and more as things turned sour with Catherine. You didn't like me then.'

'Oh but I didn't know you. But I did fancy you. You were so girly with your long hair and makeup and your stilettoes. And that skirt, so tiny. I wanted to put my hand up it.'

'How did you manage to contain yourself all these years?'

'As I told you, you seemed unattainable. But I secretly yearned.'

'Come, let's bath together. We stink of horse.

Chapter 14.

Friday and it was the conference weekend. It would be interesting to see how Martine and Jeanette fitted with my family.

They arrived in drips and drabs. Gustave had laid on a cold buffet so they could eat when they liked. The rest of the evening was spent in the salon, talking and it gave me a chance to talk to Jeanette and Martine, our latest recruits. Martine having just arrived in France seemed slightly overwhelmed. She had thought I was French, because I had picked up an accent. I assured her that I was English, at least in origin. She was a nice girl, a townie from Dalston in East London, so a voyage this early into the countryside was something of a revelation.

Jeanette proved a harder nut to crack. Although she had been in the fashion industry, she found an haute couture house very different. She wondered why we had lasted that long. Her preliminary balancing of the books showed a profit, but she asked, how had we ever achieved that if we had no real idea of what was selling profitably. Next week she said, she would be putting in input values for products, cost of material, production, transport mark up and depreciation on lines that did not sell. It all sort of made sense to me. I was glad I had appointed her, and I told her so. It seemed Simon would have run the Beauvonne fashion house into the ground. I told Jeanette that I wanted to maximise profits and eliminate losses.

Saturday morning and the conference. It went very well and served its purpose. Everyone knew what each other was doing and I outlined the aims of Maison Beauvonne. They were all on a bonus, I said, so maximum profits would be the aim. They had to start to get used to doing without me, I said, for in five months I would go back to my studies. It came as a bit of a shock. I told them that Wally would be MD in my place and Nicole Assistant MD. I would become Chairman of the Beauvonne enterprise, and keep an eye on the business overall, but day to day it would be left to them. I saw Thomas start to say something, then he stopped and settled again. When I asked for questions he remained silent.

I cornered him at buffet lunch. I asked if he was still happy at Beauvonne. He said he was, but he had been made an offer by another house and in view of Nicole and her promotion, he was seriously thinking of taking the job.

'Thomas, I need you. What does it take to retain you?'

'I just think it might be time to move on,' he said.

'I do not want to lose you. Perhaps if we give you a car to use?'

'I stay in Paris most of the time Trudi, I have no need of a car.'

'Then more money?'

'That would help. What I would really like is to take time off, say twice a year, to see what is current in New York, San Francisco and London.'

'As well as more money? I will make a bargain with you. We will pay your hotel bill in those cities, plus two thousand a year. I think that is the best I can do. Hopefully our new accountant will approve it, but you tell no one. Do you agree? You are the highest paid on our staff, except for Jacques. I really need you Thomas.'

'Very well Trudi. I stay but I could do with some help, now we have all these new lines.'

'An assistant designer, an apprentice or someone to work alongside you.'

'A junior designer, someone that knows what they are doing with knickers and bras and men's underwear. I can do it, but it is not my speciality. I am already busy with outerwear.'

'Silly of me, I should have seen that. Yes, you have more than enough to do. Do you know someone?'

'Oui, Brigitte the cutter. She has shown me some of her designs and they are brilliant.'

'I would like to see the designs and speak to her too. I will be in the Maison next week. I will talk to her.' I felt he had manoeuvred me into this and blackmailed me into giving him not only more money, but a girl friend as assistant. I was a little peeved. No one is indispensible but I hated change.

With Brigitte promoted we would have to advertise for another cutter. I consulted Jeanette on a salary. Sensibly she threw it back at me.

'Have you not thought of promoting someone to cutter and hiring a new apprentice, Madame Trudi?'

I felt a fool. Of course it was better to recruit from inside. It encouraged people if they thought there was a chance of moving up and it was much better for morale than bringing in outsiders. For a specialist like Martine, dealing with a line we had not produced before, we had to go outside and even abroad.

'Jeanette, of course, I should have thought. Then there are the demands of Thomas. What do you think?'

'To be quite honest Trudi, all I have done is to phone a recruitment agency. According to them, he is underpaid at the moment. So if you want to keep him, then you have to pay.'

'How soon Jeanette, will we have some idea of our financial position?'

'The position regarding stock will take weeks to set up. However Madame Trudi, you must have been doing something right. The salon made a net profit last year according to the auditors, of two million. When I get control of the selling prices, after analyses of costs, then I think we can improve that considerably. At the moment you are flying blind. Prices appear to have been plucked from the air. I am surprised that Maison Beauvonne still exists, but somehow it does.'

'I want to pay a bonus. The directors to have fifteen thousand each, the heads of department, cutters, head seamstresses ten and five thousand for the rest.'

'Everyone?'

'Yes, I think so. Roughly what is the total?'

'Just like that?'

'Of course you need to look into it in detail. Can you look at it urgently and give me an approximate total? If it is under three hundred thousand, then we go ahead, but we may have to adjust the amounts. I leave it with you Jeanette, but we have had a disturbing year and the staff have pulled us through. They should be rewarded. Oh and include yourself and Martine please.'

She frowned. "if that is your wish Madame, but you start these things and then they are expected every year.'

'Yes, I suppose so. I am not very good at figures Jeanette. Perhaps we should not make them so generous and we describe it as a one off, after the death of my husband, for all their help. I will have to think about future years. Let me have a rough total on those amounts and then we can adjust them as necessary. Thank you Jeanette.'

Two days later, Jeanette came up with a figure. I decided to reduce the amounts to nine thousand, six thousand and four thousand. I made no announcement,

Jeanette simply included it in their pay slips. I was rewarded with many smiling faces and thanks. I felt warm inside, but they had all been wonderful and deserved my thanks.

Two weeks later it was the show on Champ de Mars. The weather kept fine and the organisation of guest reception and coaches ferrying them worked well. The evening was warm, and everyone was merry. As dusk fell, the show got underway. It was a glittering affair, the colours of the dresses and costumes accentuated by the spotlights were spectacular, with nearly a thousand people in attendance. On this wonderful summer evening under arc lights, the show began with ready-mades, underwear, then moved to haute couture, The dogs behaved, the cat wanted to escape but its leash restrained it. None of the models fell off their heels and at the end the designers and I, including Martine, paraded the catwalk to a rousing ovation. It was a stupendous success and the newspapers next day were full of praise.

At the dinner on the following evening, I stepped back and left everything to Wally and Nicole. They did a great job, which allowed me to circulate and talk to my big family of Maison Beauvonne. At the end of the meal there started a chant of 'Trudi, Trudi.'

Eventually, goaded by Wally, I rose to my feet.

'My dear friends, my Beauvonne family. Thank you for all your hard work. My husband's death was a terrible shock to us all, and I am afraid that I felt it so greatly that I could not be much use. It has meant many changes. I have taken a year off from my studies, but will resume them in January. I will still be the owner and take an interest, but Wally will be in charge. Beauvonne is going to be a premier fashion house. The bonuses in your pay are a thank you from me and in memory of Simon. He thought the world of you and Maison Beauvonne. My husband was not a businessman, he was a country gentleman, but he loved this fashion house and he had a wonderful eye for beauty. He was kind and generous.

'I will tell you a story. In the hospital, I met a young lady who had been raped and made pregnant by her employer. I told Simon and he went to the hospital next day with bunches of flowers. Not only that, he found this young teenager work and accommodation. That is the sort of man he was.

'So in a few months, you will not see so much of me. I will be wearing jeans and a white coat, learning how to be a doctor. But I will be popping in to see you all, my big Beauvonne family. Thank you for your effort and thank you for helping me so much, not just in this year but ever since I first walked that catwalk and fell on my behind. Merci. Now, let us dance.'

They all stood and toasted me as the band struck into the first number. I danced until two. Martine and I went home together.

I undressed and washed. When I went to bed, I found Sabine there, having left the estate late and driven to Paris. I climbed in beside her and for some reason, I started to cry. It had been an emotional evening, casting off some of my responsibility.

It was wonderful to have the warmth and security of Sabine's arms around me, kissing away my tears and smoothing my hair. I fell asleep in her embrace without a sleeping pill. When I awoke, I was alone. Pinned to the pillow was a note. It simply said, 'Je t'aime Trudi.' I unpinned it and put it safely in my jewellery box.

I went to work early. Wally and Nicole were off on their tour from Friday and I wanted to make sure that all was well before they left. They were managing the New York show and it had to be a success. All seemed in order and I knew that I should not have worried, they were very competent people, but giving up the reins was more difficult than I anticipated. Perhaps I was becoming a control freak. For the next two weeks I had to be in the office while they were away. I really wanted to be at home, with the children and Sabine, riding, getting fresh air and feeling the sun on my skin. Tasha sat by my desk and followed me around as I went to speak to people.

Martine was in Clermont Ferrand and Jeanette was hardly good company. I was avoiding Thomas, still annoyed with him, probably unjustly, because he had demanded more money. Jacques was hard at work. I felt quite alone without my little assistant, Nicole. She had moved up, moved away from me and I missed her dreadfully. I made an excuse and phoned her, asking how things were going? Fine she said. And with Wally? Superb she replied. Good I said, and I meant it.

'I am missing my little assistant.'

'Oh that's a lovely thing to say. I'm sure you don't but it's nice of you to say that. Everything is going so well here, the Yanks are enthusiastic, really keen and we have all the big stores on board. Wally is so clever, he has them eating out of his hand. They just love his English accent. They think he is nobility. It is so funny. They do not like the French. I find them uncultured, well some of them. I am really enjoying myself with Wally, working hard but life is wonderful, and you have made this happen. Merci ma Princesse

For the next week I had to be in the Maison and I dreaded it.

Chapter 15.

I arrived at work with nothing really to do. As MD, it was my job to direct and to plan, that is what Simon had told me, but he was not a man of vision.

I settled at my desk with the door closed. A stack of newspapers and magazines waited to be perused for fashion news and of course anything about Beauvonne. Nicole had done this but she was not here.

I flicked through the pages, cutting anything appropriate. The Paris show reviews were excellent without exception for all the different houses, but one caught my eye in particular, which stated boldly, '**Beauvonne marchant vers l'avant'.** Beauvonne marching to the front. That was a tribute. It stated that we were still not the finished article, there were gaps in our list of merchandise, but it said, from being a down market small time haute couture house, we had become in three short years, amongst the leaders.

I opened the Mail from England, the Fashion supplement, and found unsurprisingly, that they had concentrated on my origins. They had gone back to my school, found old enemies for quotes, chased down Vanessa and my dear Sam, both of whom had short quotes in praise, but some from my old school enemies were unkind to say the least. A weird person, one said, though my teachers were full of praise. There was even a photo of the San Francisco clinic and incredibly a hazy photo of me in our garden aged about four, my hair long, down to my shoulders and I was sucking a lolly. It was not the best representation. So one of the neighbours had made a little money, ah well. The depths they had gone to ferret out the past of a nobody seemed just incredible.

In the Times I found an article by Ellie with a photo of me taken that first month in Paris, when everything was so new and I was finding my way. It was quite a nice photo, but I saw a rather gauche skinny girl, long hair half draped across my face, as if I were in hiding. I suppose I had been. The headline was 'The phenomenon that is Trudi Beauvonne.' There was a short potted history and she referred to our past friendship, saying that she had the dearest memories of watching my development into a young woman and like so many teenagers, gradually finding myself. The article was full of love, and raised guilt feelings within me. I had finally spurned her and we had gone our separate ways, she to being a big time war correspondent and me to being a fashion mogul. Memories of those days in Normandy, when Vanessa was driving me forward, introducing me to the fashion world and using me like a whore to get freebies, dresses, shoes and bags, but also responsible for my meeting Simon. My mind went back to my move to France. It had been such a traumatic time. I bit my lip and wanted to blub. How had I ever survived it all, becoming a student in one of the World's toughest regimes, where it was success or bust, right from the off. But for Élize and Jean Luc and especially Simon, I would have fallen by the wayside and returned to England. My eyes filled. Simon's photo looked sternly at me from the wall. I turned my gaze to the smiling one of us both with the children taken on the beach.

I took a deep breath. Oh Ellie, I did not love her but she was so straightforward. Get in bed and let me have fun, that was her attitude, whether I was still half male or in my female form. She did not care, yet I knew that she above any one, had really loved me and also lusted after me.

That period of my life seemed so far away now. The gradual estrangement from my parents, and my improving relationship with my brother, leaving school and moving to France with Sam, thinking she would be my companion. Horrible cruel Catherine, loomed like a nightmare. I had overcome every disadvantage with the help of Vanessa, Simon and my faithful friends. I was so lucky.

I picked up the phone and rang the Times. After giving my name, I was put through to the fashion editor. I thanked her for the article and asked for Eleanor's contact details. She promised to phone me back with them. I waited impatiently for the phone to ring. After about twenty minutes it did. To my surprise, I found Vanessa on the line.

'Trudi, c'est tu?'

There was no mistaking the voice. Vanessa who had formed me, groomed me, used me but set me ultimately on the path to success and had helped protect me from the tragedy of puberty as a boy, was on the end of the phone.

'Yes Vanessa. How are you?'

'We are fine, and I know you are from my scrapbook.'

'You keep me in a scrapbook?'

'Of course, you are like one of my own. Trudi, you wanted Ellie's number? Well she is abroad again, somewhere in the Middle East, but I will leave a message for her.'

'No don't do that. I do not want her to think I am searching her out for, well you know how it was with her and me. I do not want to go back to that. That must sound conceited, she probably regrets her fling with me now. I have just read her article in the Times and memories came flooding back of her and you and your family. I have not seen you since the wedding, and then I did not see you enough.'

'You were so busy, I hardly recognised the little waif I first dressed in Lincolnshire and sent you out to be a whore. I am so ashamed.'

'Don't be. I think of you in the dearest way, you did so much for me. But for you I would be a sad little shy person trying to live down my past, not the Comtesse, owner of Beauvonne with three lovely children. Your family is my family.'

'But Trudi, I keep thinking back to the time we discovered you were a girl, and how I used you. I am so ashamed.'

'I do not know how I carried that off. With the awful Tom? I think it was the adrenalin trip I was on that day when you discovered the real me and I became, from that time, the real me. It was that dreadful evening as a courtesan on the arm of a repulsive man, that convinced me I could actually succeed at becoming what I have become. And afterwards, you were so generous and yes a bit naughty too. It was all just part of my journey, so don't feel ashamed. Have you been in France this summer?'

'No, with the children grown up it would have been just me rattling around in that old house alone. I felt I was better off here.'

'Then come and stay with me, in two weeks time I will have a week in the chateau. It will be fun. But I have some news too. I think you met Sabine at the wedding. Perhaps you don't remember?"

'I think so, with your friend Wally?'

'Yes. They have parted. Sabine was in love with someone else, in fact with me. The result is that we are seeing if we can be a couple. I am telling you this because if you are coming, then I want no pretence.'

'You didn't ring me to tell me that Trudi? I mean you can make your own mind up about such things and you know nothing much shocks me.'

'No. I rang to tell Ellie how wonderful her piece in the Times on me was and say thank you. I was overcome. Look, if you are free, say you will come and stay. Sabine will be working on the harvest, so I will have plenty of time to be with you and you can get to know my children. This is a once in a lifetime chance for us to have time together. Next year I shall be back in the hospital. Please come Vanessa?'

'You have persuaded me Trudi. I will be with you a week next Monday.' We chatted on. Stuart was expecting his second child. Thoughts flew through my mind of the day he made me blow him, had my ears pierced and taken me out in his sisters clothes, the same day that Vanessa had discovered me as a girl. Had Stuart been homosexual or did he really see the girl within me. I would never know. I could never forget his later rape too.

Claire was still at university, doing a doctorate in philosophy. That alone seemed unreal. She had been such a brat. I asked if she would like to come with her mother, but no, she was off train hopping to Eastern Europe with a boyfriend.

I put the phone down and continued with the newspapers and mags. Buried in the inner pages of Paris Soir was a short article on Paul Morel. The case had been dropped. He had received a police warning.

It was enough. He had taken me for fifteen thousand, the price of buying back a favourite painting and two hundred and fifty thousand for Franco's friends. If I had gone through the courts it would have taken years and millions of euros. I smiled, wondering how Paul had felt on drugs, dressed as a down at heel whore, sitting amongst the other flotsam of Paris in the police station. He must have woken very confused. I flushed with guilt. He had also lost everything, Antoinette told me, his law practice failed and he was working in a walk in law centre.

A knock at the door broke the mood. Brigitte entered all smiles with a number of designs for underwear. They were very pretty, very lovely indeed.

'Let us talk sizing Brigitte. These little things are not going to suit anyone with a bust measurement over 96 cms. So we only make sizes up to that. We are not able to appeal to fatties, it is just not economical. So limited sizing, in your four designs, the range will not be too formidable.

'What you now have to do, is present Jeanette with all your costings. Materials, machining times, storage and transport, our profit and a selling price giving the retailer at least 40%, if we make them here in France which I would rather do. She will help you.

'But also, you should find about four manufacturers from the East, China, Indonesia, India, and get costings from them, to make and ship. Go to Clermont Ferrand and speak to George about making costs. So far you have done the easy part. Now is the hard graft. Speak to Martine and see when she next goes to Clermont and you can go together. Well done on the designs. I like them a lot and can't wait to wear them myself.'

'Merci Trudi.' They were very pretty. I finished the media reading. Then I picked up my bag and went on a tour of the building, speaking to as many as possible, trying to remember all their names. We had nearly over a hundred working here and another two hundred in Clermont Ferrand, so it was difficult to remember all their names.

I was talking to a junior seamstress, Lucie. She was a bright girl with a ring in her nose. I could not keep my eyes from it. She was a very pretty little thing and I should have admired her bright clear skin, eyes and features, yet my eyes seemed riveted on that self imposed blemish.

She looked at me cheekily. I asked what she was working on. She showed me the rolled hem of a full silk evening skirt. The tiny stitches were evenly spaced.

'That's very neat work Lucie. What do you hope to do here?

'To be a designer one day.'

'A career girl? What about marriage and children?'

'Maybe that too. But you manage to do so many things, why shouldn't I?'

'Ah touché Lucie. There is no reason at all if you are ambitious.'

'You keep looking at the ring Madame, do you not approve?'

'It is your nose and you may do with it as you like Lucie. In my opinion, you are a very pretty girl, and that thing diverts my eyes from admiring your elfin face and beautiful eyes. You don't need it. However it is your business. So you want to be a designer? Of what, shoes, bags, dresses?'

'I can show you.'

She carefully inserted the needle in her next stitch, leaving it wedged safely there and pushed the silk aside. She pulled a satchel from under her table, undid the flap and took out a sheaf of papers, laying them out. Amongst them were some very attractive designs, though some were hardly original.

'So are these your spare time doodles or are you serious?'

'I am going to school after work. I don't think they are doodles Madame,' she said indignantly. 'I want to be rich and have nice things like you.'

'Good. I am glad you are a serious girl. I like your spirit. When do you go to lunch Lucie?'

'I don't. I cannot afford lunch and my classes on my pay here.'

'Today, I am free for lunch. Would you like to have lunch with me. Oh yes, I will pay.'

'Oui madame, merci.'

I went into Jacques office. It was untidy as usual, with discarded designs thrown towards the bin. His two drawing boards showed designs that might make it to production. Each night the floor was cleared and the discards shredded so that they were not pirated.

'Trudi, what can I do for you?'

'How would you like an apprentice Jacques?'

'What do you mean?'

'I have just been speaking to Lucie, the young seamstress. She is studying design and I thought one or two designs were rather good. I wonder whether you would consider taking her under your wing, coach her and encourage her and perhaps, if she produces something worthwhile, we could make it up for the next show. What do you think?'

'Where would I put her? This office is small as it is.'

'When we have the next door premises, there will be a whole new design suite on the first floor. Your office will be three times the size. Jacques, come to lunch with me and this girl and see if you can work with her. We have to train and encourage our own people.'

'Why have I not heard about this new space before Trudi?'

'Because we only looked at it two weeks ago and we are negotiating for it. But you will of course be fully consulted on the design and decoration.'

'Lucie. She is that funny little girl with the nose ring. Well there is no harm in seeing her. Of course we can have lunch Trudi. At what time?'

'Leave here at ten to one Jacques. Meet at the door.'

I booked a restaurant for four, asking Thomas to come as well. Martine and Brigitte were in Clermont, otherwise I would have asked them too.

When Lucie appeared, I found she had removed the nose ring. It improved her greatly. She was quite fashionable in a slightly punky way. Perhaps this was what we needed.

Was Jacques becoming too staid I wondered as we walked to Villa Spicy.

We entered and I saw a good many from the fashion world that I knew. I spoke to one or two, Marco, who had given me shoes and I had modelled for. Pierre who fancied me when I was still a boy in drag, and who I had slept with in return for a wardrobe of designer clothes. It seemed a long, long time ago. My small party moved to a back room where we could talk in private.

To my surprise Jacques was quite charming to Lucie and they were soon joking and laughing. Thomas was cheerful and full of his plans. He hinted that he and Martine were seeing each other. I did not take the bait and ask for details. When the sweets came, Jacques said to Lucie, 'Would you like to work with me Lucie?'

'Doing what Monsieur Jacques?'

'Designing Lucie, isn't that what you aspire to do?'

'You mean actually designing for the show?'

'If you have something good, yes. We do not say that everything you think up will end on the catwalk. You will be an apprentice. You go to study, not at night but two days a week. Study hard and work hard. Maybe I can learn something from you while you learn from me.'

'Lucie,' I said, 'this is a great opportunity. Too much attitude and it ends here. Jacques will be your boss and what he says is law. If you upset him, you upset me and it all ends. Now I see in you a great spirit and a young eye. I think we need a little radical design. If you can give us something, then you will progress. If not you return to the sewing room I leave it to you. Do you want this opportunity?'

'Of course Madame. Thank you and Monsieur Jacques aussi.'

'Good we are pleased to have you. At the moment there is no room for you with Jacques but within a month, I hope we will have more room and you can have a board with the designers. You will have two days at fashion college paid by us and three days in the office. We will pay you the same money, but if you prove that you can design, then we will review your salary. And show respect, you will be with some of the best people in this industry. Do we have a deal?'

'Of course Madame. Merci.' She blushed. As we walked home I felt a tug on my sleeve.

'Madame Trudi? I am sorry for my attitude. I come from a tough area, a tough school. If you don't show attitude you get beat up.'

"OK Lucie, but we are civilised people, we want to help you. Neither Jacques nor I will put up with rudeness. By the way, you look very pretty without that nose ring, really.'

'Merci Madame Trudi. I can do this. I am really a nice person.'

'I thought so, that is why I am giving you this chance.'

Chapter 16.

I left for Beauvonne early Friday afternoon and was home by five in time to play with the children. Sabine, Sophie and I had dinner, then watched TV. We went to bed early. I told Sabine that Vanessa would be spending two weeks with me from Monday.

'I shall be busy Trudi, dawn till dusk. They start on the winter barley on Monday, and follow on with the rape. So I won't have a minute.'

'I know, that is partly why I have asked her. She is one of my oldest friends, the reason I am in France. I have told her about us, said we are in love and seeing if it will work out. So we don't pretend at all.'

She grinned. It was a very boyish look. If it had not been for her girlie pink flowered PJs, I could almost have thought her a boy. 'Ma brave Trudi! Bon, I am glad you will have company.'

'You know it was Vanessa's daughter Eleanor who was my first female lover?'

'A long time ago. Are you trying to make me jealous?'

'Oh no, nothing like that, no Sabine never.'

'I am teasing Trudi. Your past means nothing to me.'

'This is what she wrote about me.' I handed her the cutting from the Times.

'You know I am not good at English Trudi. If you want me to know what it says, you have to translate.'

I did so.

'So she still loves you,' she said.

'I think so. But I never loved her Sabine. I was just a plaything then uncertain of myself, even afraid of her. I just don't want secrets at all. Simon knew everything about me. That was why our relationship worked. I want us to be the same.'

'You worry too much Trudi, ma chérie. Go to sleep. I have to be up early.'

I fell asleep holding her in my arms and awoke to find myself alone.

The door burst open and the children rushed in, climbing up on the bed with difficulty. I pulled Sébastien up, and submitted to their wet kisses. Tasha shot in chased by Mitzi followed by a breathless Sophie.

'I'm sorry Trudi, they escaped while I was dressing. How are you?'

'Ça ne fait rien. I was awake Sophie. Take them down to breakfast and I will be down soon. Who wants to go to the sea?'

They all shouted, Sébastien copying his brother and sister. Tasha jumped on the bed to add to the mêlée. I pulled myself from the covers with difficulty, heaving hot little bodies carefully off me.

We were about to leave for the seaside when Wally and Nicole arrived, returned from their tour and going to the house which Wally was to have shared with Sabine had they married. The children crowded round Nicole, and she bent and kissed each one.

'Wally, why don't we go to the sea too? It would be so relaxing and fun.'

'If you like darling.' He looked at me. 'Is that all right Trudi?'

'Of course, it will be fun if you both want to. We shall not be too late back, because these little ones will be in bed by seven. Let me buy lunch, then all you have to do, is have a snack tonight. Is your house habitable? Has it been aired and made ready?'

'Well no, we sort of thought to camp out and plan what we were going to do with it, well Nicole wants to make some changes anyway.'

'I haven't even seen it, so naturally I want to have my say.'

'Look stay here tonight, then go over to the house tomorrow. That will be much more sensible. And you know, while things are being done and you need to keep an eye on it, you can always stay here. Come on, say yes.'

'I hoped you would say that,' Nicole said.

'Then why on earth did you not ask outright?'

'Well, there is Sabine to think of.'

'Yes of course. But I think Sabine will say, she has the better part of the bargain. She will not mind. She and I are fine and certainly happy. And we are all family. Besides, I am taking two weeks off, so you can tell me all about your trip and I can fill you in on what has happened while you were away. I have an old friend staying from Monday for two weeks, the woman who first brought me to France as a gauche little fifteen year old. This is our chance to catch up.'

'It's settled then. We'll stay with you Trudi. Thank you.'

I could see that Nicole was the boss. In some ways Wally was very easy going.

At the beach, I had a chance to walk with him while Nicole and Sophie had a sisterly chat and amused the children.

'So how was your trip?'

'Very successful. We have a full order book, the most business we have ever done. The bags are in demand, but we could not make promises on them. We have taken orders but have not made promises, just that we would do our best. New York loved the new readymade suits, So did Tokyo. And Dubai went mad for haute couture dresses and funnily enough, men's underwear.'

'That is great Wally. And Nicole, did she find the trip useful?'

'What are you wanting to know Trudi.' He fixed me with his quizzical look.

'Well first of all, did she make contacts?'

'Oh sure, yes she will tell you all about that. She did well, she is exceptionally clever. Remembers everyone's name which I find hard.'

'While you were away, I appointed an apprentice designer. I don't know whether you know Lucie, a little punk girl seamstress? She showed me some designs she had done and she is studying design. Jacques is taking her under his wing. Oh and next week we should hear about the premises next door, so you two keep an eye on that. I have a prospective builder to make the alterations. We need the room urgently Wally.'

'OK. You will only be a phone call away. Will you bring Vanessa to Paris?'

'I think so, at some time. She used to be a model.'

'Not Stuart's mum?'

'Yes Wally, the same.'

'What's that creep doing now?'

'He is very successful in the agri business, expecting his second child.'

'Have you seen him?'

'Not since our wedding and then only for a minute. His sister Ellie still loves me. Wrote a piece in the Times on me. I'll show you tonight.'

'You're a bit of a magnet aren't you Trudi!'

'That is enough about me. Anyway, your tour was successful. And personally Wally, how was it with my Nicole? You may as well tell me and stop being coy.'

'Well you know I don't talk about such things, but in this case, yes this is the real thing. I have never felt like this about anyone before. I can't take my eyes off her and just want to hold her close.'

'She seems happy. So the undemonstrative Englishman has gone? You really have found what love is all about? There was a time Wally when I felt you didn't know how to love, except I thought you loved me a bit, I mean in a brotherly way.'

'At school, first off thought you were weird but harmless. Later I thought you vulnerable and did not like the whispering and bullying.'

'What whispering? When?'

'Oh before the dramatic change. You were so girlie.'

'I thought I hid myself rather well.'

He laughed. 'Well your finger nails for a start and your eyebrows, your hair! You looked like a girl playing the part of a boy in some amateur production. Too clean, too pristine, little white shirts manicured nails. It was still a surprise when you walked in dressed as a girl, but somehow right. Like Blackadder and Bob, he couldn't understand the strange stirrings in his loins for 'Bob'. It was the same for us really. But I could see that you had tried to be what you were not, a boy, and I admired you for trying. So yes, I took a brotherly interest.'

'Well it was all pretty strange for me. I was so self absorbed trying to fit in, I hardly considered the effect I had on people around me.' I reached for his hand and kissed him on the cheek. 'I think I was a bit in love with you, big, strong, protective. It was easy to sort of daydream. Simon thought I was in love with you, not as a rival to him but, well attracted. I don't believe there will ever be another Simon in my life, no other man. No I think I shall be very happy with Sabine. Anyway, you and Nicole, I am so glad. I love Nicole. She has above anyone been my soul mate, confidant, pal, girl friend and gofer. I told her it was a good day when she stood waiting for me in Moutier. So all is well in the world of Beauvonne?'

'As far as we are concerned, yes. We worked hard but it was easy because we were both so happy.'

'Oh Wally I am so pleased for you both.'

'And you and Sabine?'

'Oh, well it is different. But yes, I think we are fine. It is early days. When I am in Paris I miss her and I am excited to get home. It is her busy time, so we have not had that much time together. She loves me a great deal and for me, it is easy, easy for me to love her and let her love me. I feel more relaxed with Sabine than I have been with anyone, even with Simon. No I am very happy. Now I want to get back to my studies and you and Nicole have to fill my shoes and make decisions. I am tired of it and frankly a little bored. I know that does not sound right, but I had a vision for Beauvonne, while Simon just wanted to jog along. In this world one has to progress, to grow or one withers. I feel my vision is now fulfilled, but the vision needs to be developed and that is for you and Nicole. That does not mean that I will just walk away into the sunset, but day-to-day I expect you to manage. I have the estate and my medical career and above all the beloved children to look after.'

'You can count on us Trudi. Comtesse de Beauvonne. I never thought at school that things would have turned out this way. It's good to be part of your story and we both love you.'

'Thanks Wally. We had better get back and play. I have booked a table for two o'clock. We'll have a leisurely lunch and get home in time to put the children in the bath. A spot of tea, then we can relax for the evening.'

We spent two hours building a sand castle, and made our way to the restaurant. We ate seafood, great mixed platters of lobster, spider crab, mussels and crispy plaice, with chips and salad. We finished off with fruit tarts and ice cream.

At the Chateau Nicole, Wally and I put the children in the bath and had a wonderful time with them, splashing, singing songs and washing. We pulled them out swaddled in towels and dried their hair. We took them downstairs in their PJs. I carried Sébastien, loving the feel of his hot little body against mine. After tea I put them to bed, reading 'Where is my elephant?' I tucked them up, kissed them and went down to the salon. Sophie had gone out with Laurent.

Sabine came in dusty and dirty at nine. I got her dinner and then we two went to bed. We showered together and made love in the shower. She was very strong, bending me to her will but she was also tender and loving. I giggled a lot. In bed, we fell asleep almost immediately, cuddled together. It had been a really good day.

Chapter 17.

I awoke in time to kiss Sabine as she went to work. I would not see her until evening unless she could find time for lunch. She promised to keep her phone on and I proposed to take her a picnic wherever she might be on the estate.

When she had gone, I bathed and dressed quickly and made for the nursery. I found the children playing while Sophie was showering and dressing. I proceeded to wash and dress Sébastien first and then the twins. They were so adorable, such happy children. Of course they fought with each other at times, over possession of toys or turns, but most of the time they were the best of pals. I did not understand how their real mother could have been so indifferent to them. Simon had been a somewhat distant father too until I had involved him. Then he had understood what fatherhood was really about. It was seven months since his death and the children never spoke of him. When they were older, I would tell them about him. In the meantime I was making an album about their father, so they would understand where they came from. I made a separate book for Catherine, leaving out most of the critical articles, but I had to also tell them the truth.

I could not have loved them more had they been my own. I resolved that when I resumed my medical studies, they would move to Paris with me, returning to Beauvonne only when I had two or three days leave. I wanted them close to me, wanted to be their maman, to give them as normal an upbringing as possible. There would inevitably be a strain on my relationship with Sabine, but if I am to become a doctor, then concessions have to be made. I could be parted from her for five or six days. Would she be content with such an arrangement? I would have to discuss it with her.

Sunday I was alone with the children. Sophie had gone to Laurent's farm although he was working on their harvest and of course, Sabine was busy. We amused ourselves with the ponies and made a picnic for Sabine, cold chicken and salad with fruit juices. She greeted us, dust covered, her clean blue shirt quite grey in the folds. I was worried that she was ingesting dust, but she assured me that she wore a mask when necessary.

Back in the Chateau, we four readied a room for Vanessa. The children were like kittens, trying to dive under the falling sheet and tugging on the corners to tuck them in. I was bathing them when Sophie returned and she immediately helped me out. I read them a story, we sang two songs and after kisses, I went down to the study to write an email to Wally about our future path.

Sabine didn't come in until after nine. The winter barley had been completed, but the yield was only average. However, the oil seed rape was extremely good and the spring wheat was looking promising. We were in bed and cuddled up by ten.

In the morning Sabine was again up and ready to go by the time I roused myself. I bathed and dressed carefully, knowing that Vanessa would see me with her critical eyes. She was flying into Charles de Gaulle at midday and getting the train to Chartres where I would pick her up just after two.

Sophie had taken the children to play school, so I had a quiet time. I wrote to my brother in Afghanistan and to my parents hoping that they would check their emails.

Vanessa's imminent arrival was stirring so many memories of that time when I had been the little transvestite. I suddenly felt quite angry at the way I had been used. Vanessa had blackmailed Tom after he had taken me out and then used me to obtain 'goodies' from the fashionistas. When I was so vulnerable she had allowed Stuart and Ellie to pursue me.

Even Simon had used me as a mistress. Catherine consequently had hated me. And there was Catherine's mysterious death. I had no idea of the truth only what beloved Simon had told me. Had he actually killed her, even if it was manslaughter? And that creep Paul. Sabine was the only honourable lover. She had never used me, on the contrary, she had been quite rude to me until she recognised that I was not just a bimbo.

Perhaps I had been too easily manipulated by these people. I flushed as I thought about Stuart's rape and Dirty David the tennis coach. I wondered how he had ever removed that lock from his genitals. I was so unsure of my place in the

World that I had allowed them to do with me as they liked. Suddenly I laughed. Whatever they had done, I had come out on top. Sometimes I wreaked a terrible revenge.

I thought about Simon as I stared out of the window, seeing the combines working away at the winter wheat in the distance and watching as Sabine's Land Rover bumped towards them. The tractors with their trailers ran back and forth to the barn, emptying their loads and returning for another. Tasha pawed at my knee wanting attention. Maybe I had been a little gauche, a puppet on the end of strings, but I had gradually assumed character and become as Wally said, 'une femme formidable'. Now I had an empire, and articles in the Times about my achievements rather than about my traumatic sex life. Three hundred people worked under my direction. Oh yes I had inherited Simon's wealth, but I had turned his business around with my ideas, my drive and ambition. I was halfway qualified as a physician too. And in six weeks time I would be twenty-five.

I got up and checked myself in the mirror. I saw a good looking woman with good legs, dressed in a classic cap sleeved cream shirtwaister dress. I was pleased with my appearance. I had become what I aspired to be. If I had a magic wand, would I have wished to start again from birth as a girl? Perhaps. No certainly. To have a fully working female body would have been wonderful, but I am what I am and that is a good deal better than most have in a lifetime. I had been extremely lucky and for all her faults, Vanessa had set me on this path to success. She above anyone had seen the potential in me, from the very first time I walked into her kitchen dressed in Eleanor's cast off clothing. I bore her no grudge at all.

I took the new Peugeot to Chartres driving easily below the speed limit. The train was on time. I greeted Vanessa at the station door, took her heavy suitcase and stowed it in the back.

'Have you eaten Vanessa?'

'No, I have not had anything except some rather doubtful coffee.'

'Then I suggest that we go to the Rive Droite in Alençon. I'll give them a ring.' I phoned and booked a table for a late lunch.

As I drove Vanessa chattered away about the family. Stuart was proving a good farmer. Claire was still doing her philosophy doctorate, 'a real swot', Vanessa said, disapprovingly. 'Oh you should see her, tangled hair and torn jeans darling. Simply deplorable. Not like you at all. You could have just stepped out of Vogue.'

'And Ellie? How is she, where is she?'

'Oh I don't know. Mali or Nigeria or somewhere, always on the move. I shudder when she tells me anything and she leaves out the worst, but she has quite a reputation. Very much in demand. Sky approached her, and the Beeb, but she wants to remain freelance, her own boss, and with her rep, she can demand her own price and choose where she goes. I read that piece she did on you. She still holds a torch doesn't she.'

'I am afraid so, Vanessa, but I don't love her though I am very fond.'

'This Sabine must be rather special darling, if you love her. So how long has this been going on?'

I told her the whole story, finishing just as we parked.

We entered Rive Droite and received a lovely welcome from Bertrand.

'They love you here don't they Comtesse. My gauche little Trudi, how innocent and malleable you were. Now such une grande femme. I congratulate you.'

'Wally calls me une femme formidable.'

'I am not surprised. You have a good head on your shoulders. And I am not entirely surprised about Sabine. I always thought that what held you back from giving yourself to Eleanor, was shyness and embarrassment more than anything. Now you exude confidence. Anyway, I am pleased that you have found somebody to share your life with. And what else have you been up to?'

I went through all the changes I had made at Maison Beauvonne and our plans for the future. I said I was going back to my studies in five months time.

'I'm surprised that you still want to study. You have the World at your feet, yet you want to deal with horrible things in hospital. It is as bad as becoming a nun having once been a film star. What are you going to specialise in?'

'It is too early to say as I have not covered all the disciplines yet. There are so many areas that need good doctors. There are more like me who need understanding treatment, or oncology or plastic surgery for people who really need it, to correct birth defects or the results of some dreadful accident. I don't know, there are so many areas, all are worthwhile. There is Médicins sans Frontiere, working in disaster areas. That is all for the future. I am going to see whether I can do all my study in a four-day week, so I can have a long weekend with Sabine and the children. I'm hoping that Professor Rousse will support my request.'

'You do sound dedicated darling Trudi. I cannot say it's a waste, but the medical profession will be lucky to have you. All I will say is that compared with the little girl-boy I brought to France, well in fact there is no comparison. You are now not a pretty woman but a beautiful woman. Your looks have changed completely, I suppose the hormones have had a terrific effect. Even since last year at the wedding, yes you took my breathe away then, but today, darling you are a star. I wish I could tell everyone that you are my daughter. You could earn a fortune as a full time model and maybe go on to films. If I had been as beautiful as you, my modelling career would have paid far more than the farm. I should never have become a farmer's wife at twenty-six and pregnant at twenty-eight.'

'When I met you, you were what, forty-two?'

'Going on forty-four, darling.'

'I thought you the most beautiful and sophisticated lady I had ever seen. I worshipped you from the first time I shook your hand and I wanted to be like you. That's partly why I tried on your dresses, although they were really divine. And when we went to church, you wore a navy suit with a little pillbox hat with a yellow band. I thought it was exquisite. You were my role model. Audrey Hepburn could not have influenced me more.'

'Oh Trudi, thank you. You have not lost your sweetness. Sabine is a lucky woman.'

'I was lucky to meet you. Indirectly you introduced me to Simon, at that fancy dress party. Do you remember? I was feeling shy and had moved away from the crowd and suddenly a man in riding gear was chatting to me. I thought he was in fancy dress until he showed me his horse and the Chateau, way across the fields next to the forest. Then you took me to that professor who supplied me with drugs to stop male puberty. That probably saved my life. If I had grown facial hair and my voice had dropped......., I don't think I could have coped.'

'Well, I did owe you for Tom and how I had taken advantage of you. But I saw great potential in you. I have also to confess, that I got quite a kick out of changing you into a lady. I felt quite powerful. It was almost sexual, I mean the pleasure I got from doing it. I made you walk in the bedroom until your deportment was that of a sophisticated lady. And I gave you to Pierre for designer clothes. That was truly dreadful. Yet here we are. It just proves that all that sort of thing, sex really isn't important. It is emotions that count.'

I looked at her. I suddenly woke up to the fact that she was quite amoral and completely selfish. Everything she had done for me was as much for herself at least. It was of no matter. Whatever her motives in changing me, she had done what I wanted her to do, and I had profited from her attentions. Sometimes, rarely, I had to pay a price. Most women do, don't they, in one way or another? She and Simon had moulded me into a lady, taught me so much, but Simon had done it out of love. Vanessa seemed to have done it for her own gratification. I let it pass.

'I have much to thank you for Vanessa, even if you were a bit naughty. Now what am I going to do with you for the next two weeks? What do you want to do?'

'I would love to go to Paris and see what you are doing there. And do you remember my favourite place at the beach, the secluded beach with the trees where we often picnicked? I would love to go there too.'

'Of course, but we have to take the children too. I need to spend time with them. We can ride, the horses never get enough exercise. I have a groom to exercise them but with Sabine so busy, she and I do not ride enough.'

'Oh that sounds wonderful. Of course you need time with your children Trudi. It will be delightful.'

'Then this week we spend in Normandy and next week, well Sunday we can all take off for Paris. Sophie will entertain the children so we have time to shop, and I hope that Maison Beauvonne will be expanding into the next-door premises. Oh and I didn't tell you about our factory in Clermont Ferrand. We won't go there but it is an essential part of our organisation. I don't like placing orders with the sweatshops of the Far East and I want to employ French people to make French goods.'

'Trudi, you are as moral as Mother Teresa.'

'I haven't always been so. I have done some quite awful things.'

'I don't believe you Trudi.'

'Well I have, but that was mostly in my distant past. But if crossed, I can be very ruthless. Wally calls me Madame Machiavelli, but maybe I am more like Madame Borgia.'

We had eaten our way through four courses. 'Come Vanessa, time to go to the Chateau. We will be in time to bathe the children and put them to bed.'

On the drive, she told me about Claire. She was a disappointment she said. Dressed like a tramp and her head always in a book. That was not Vanessa's dream for her daughter. One daughter was roving the World's hot spots looking like a man, the other a student with no sense of fashion. Her son, who had raped me, was a successful but clod hopping farmer. None of her values had passed to her children. As far as they were concerned, all her dreams for them were shattered. While Stuart's father had been a farmer and a gentleman, Stuart was a clever farmer but a lumbering oaf by what she said. He had not changed then. If she only knew the truth, she would be devastated. Poor Vanessa.

Chapter 18.

We had a very good start to the week. Vanessa was excellent with the children, so Sophie took off to see her parents for a few days, to return Friday night. Vanessa and I rode only once, on the first afternoon, but we took the children out on their ponies. We spent a lot of time at the beach and in various restaurants. Vanessa made me laugh, more than I had laughed for a long time. She was no longer the daunting older woman to me, but an equal and she was truly outrageous in some of her observations. I giggled and rocked at her descriptions of her farming acquaintances and her tales from her time on the catwalk. The truth was that a relatively rich farmer had wooed and won her, but she was not a country-woman, nor would she become one. Vanessa truly was a foreigner up there in the wastes of Lincolnshire, surrounded by dykes and no hill in sight.

In my past, she had been like a goddess. Vanessa now was quite uninhibited. She taught me to polka on the beach, bare footed, the children racing around us and with Tasha skipping between our feet. Everything turned into a game. My stocks of cheap champagne dwindled, yet she never seemed drunk, just merry.

Yet all the while she was very attentive to the children, reading to them, telling stories from history, King Richard, the so called Lion Heart, who deserted his Kingdom, leaving evil King John in charge while Richard went to fight in the Crusades. And a sort of potted Dickens, A Tale of Two Cities, of aristocrats having their heads cut off and the Scarlet Pimpernel rescuing them. She made the stories frightening and funny at the same time and the children were rapt, seeing the whole thing in their minds, clinging to us when frightened and rocking and giggling when it was funny. She called them the Three Musketeers and gave a children's version of the court and international intrigue in that book. She certainly knew how to tell a story. It was the best, most intimate time I had experienced with the children. They threw themselves at me and I loved it.

She examined my wardrobe, picking out items that she admired. She watched the video of our last show and was genuinely impressed.

Sabine was out most of the time. Some fields were being ploughed up, immediately after harvest. Others would be left fallow and planted in the spring. It was a sure sign of summer's passing. She took Wednesday off and came with us. While I dug a moat and built a huge castle with the children, Sabine and Vanessa walked away up the beach. I knew they would be discussing me, but I was sure enough of them and myself to be relaxed about it. They came back laughing.

'I approve,' Vanessa said in English, 'Sabine is all you said she was, and she really loves you Trudi.' Sabine stood back, listening.

'Sabine does understand English you know Vanessa, and that is not really news to us.' I took Sabine's hand. 'I love her too. We are comfortable with each other and she excites me and I know I excite her. It couldn't have worked out better.'

I kissed Sabine and was aroused. The children danced around us. 'Come children,' I said, 'see that big rock on the beach? Ice creams if you beat me to it. Prêt, partez.' We ran giggling, the children competing with each other, André making sure Adèle came second by running in front of her. Breathless we collapsed, all in a heap. We sang on the way home, stopping for ice creams at our favourite shop.

We all shared supper of cold meat and crab with salad. It had been a beautiful day, maybe my best day ever. Simon seemed suddenly a distant sorrow. I bit my lip as I thought of him, but no tears came at least. The future seemed brighter. I was beginning to see through all the problems and trials of managing my empire, to my future life as a mother and a doctor. Vanessa, Sabine and I sat up late chatting. It was embarrassing hearing stories about myself from my distant past, but Sabine sat with me and squeezed my hand reassuringly.

I drifted off into memories of those early days, that first holiday with Vanessa in France. I was brought back with a jolt when I heard her asking, 'Have you no regrets at all?'

'Do you have regrets about your life Vanessa? I suspect you do. Don't most people? After all, we are only human, an intelligent animal on this planet. A cow may look enviously at the grass over the fence. Humans are similar but much more complicated.'

'Yes but I was asking you?'

'Few people have perfect lives. By accident of birth, I had my defect, which I have done my best to correct. But sexuality, is at the base of anyone's character. It was a constant hurt from as early as I can remember. Mother first did her best to make me feel like a boy, and then made a compromise, so that I was half and half and finally, I became as close as possible to what I wanted to be. Oh yes, I can let myself regret, cry *I am a victim,* but my life has great compensations that other *normal* people don't have. My appreciation of being a girl, a woman, is far higher than that of most women, because I know the converse. And I have been very lucky, born with a brain. I was taken home by Stuart and discovered by you and of course, that led to meeting Simon. It could all have been so much worse. I could have ended up on the street or pole dancing, or scrubbing floors. Some with my condition, kill themselves. Regrets, of course I have them, but on balance, I call myself fortunate. But you Vanessa, you do have regrets don't you/'

'Well not really.'

'Your children, all three are not what you would have them be. Stuart does not have the manners of his father. Ellie looks like a boy and Claire lives the life of a Bohemian. In some ways, you would rather they were like me. You ought to be proud of Ellie, at the top of her profession and Claire too, must have a good brain even if you do not appreciate what she does and how she looks. Stuart too is successful.'

'He is the biggest disappointment. I know he lusted after you and I suspect that his expulsion was something to do with that. He never smoked cannabis in his life.'

'What happened back then was something else. I think he found me intriguing, first as a boy and then as a girl. He could not understand it and somehow my androgyny attracted him. When I came to you I had no idea that he had feelings for me, other than as une amie.' I realised that I had said too much.

'And you lied when we asked if anything was going on between you, when you stood looking so pretty in our kitchen in Ellie's dress.'

'Oh yes he fancied me, encouraged me after he discovered me cross-dressed. If you had not returned, I do not know what would have happened. We might have kissed, I don't know. He had thought it a wheeze to take me out dressed as a girl, a dare to me. Of course it was no such thing as at home I was always a girl. That is all that happened. I must have been very androgynous. When John picked us up from the station, he even spoke to me as though I was a girl. I liked it. It was a vindication of how I felt about myself. Stuart had to remind him that I wasn't a girl. It was probably just as confusing for all of you as it was for me. John strongly disapproved of me, didn't he?'

'I wouldn't say that. He was shocked and worried about Stuart and what was really going on between you.'

'Well the answer to that is, nothing. We were sort of mates at school for a time, but we had nothing in common. We shared a study for a year and he was so into farming and driving tractors, teaching me how to reverse with a trailer. I was just not bothered. We sort of gradually grew apart after our first holiday in France. He tended to tease and it was not something I wanted to be teased about. I am sure he was not using drugs. I think someone had stashed drugs in his room to protect themselves. One minute he was at school, the next he had gone.'

I put the news on and heard more about Afghanistan. More deaths of British servicemen. It worried me. Soon after, we went to bed.

With the light out, snuggled together Sabine said, 'What were you hiding from her?'

'Sabine, from you I do not hold secrets. Stuart got me drunk and raped me. My friends planted the drugs and he was consequently expelled. Actually I think we did him a favour. How did you know?'

'I know you Trudi, ma Comtesse. I know you, and I love you, but I know that when you are threatened, you can be ruthless. What really happened with Stuart?

I told her the whole story, even having to go back right into childhood and my double life. When I reached the visit to Stuart's home and related my dressing in Vanessa's clothes, she giggled. I told her about Tom and how she had used me in Paris to obtain freebies.

'Why is this woman in your house?' she asked.

'Because I owe her everything. But for her I would not have come to France, I would not have obtained the drugs I needed. I would not have met Simon, who paid for my surgery. I would not have been in Paris to study, would not have met you, would not have three lovely children. This is why I forgive her. The price I paid was little compared to the benefits received. What is a bit of unrequited sex? It is nothing.'

'You can be so logical. Is this nothing? You and me. Are we real?'

'I chose you. I did not have to. I love you Sabine and I want you here with me. Now kiss me.'

She made love to me, quite savagely at first, gradually calming and becoming gentle. She loved my breasts, loved to cup them in her hands. Eventually we fell asleep wrapped in each other.

Over the next two days Vanessa and I amused the children. Sophie returned on Saturday. Sunday was a brilliant day and Sabine was free. We all met Wally and Nicole at the Rive Droite for a long lunch. It was a brilliant time until the coffee.

Vanessa was sat next to Wally in the lounge. From a distance I heard her say, 'So you knew Stuart?'

'Oh yes Stuart. Yes I knew him. We were in the same form, but not in the same gang. I was studying hard and playing hard. I always thought Stuart's attention was at home, with the farm and his cars and machinery.'

'So he was a sort of outsider?'

'A one off. School wasn't the place for him. He was centred on farming.'

'And in love with Trudi,' she said as though it was fact.

'Well, a bit obsessed, when she changed.'

'I know,' I heard Vanessa saying while Nicole was trying to tell me about her house renovations. 'So you had to do something to stop him, I understand.'

Desperately I tried to catch Wally's eye and just for a second, he saw me, then looked away. I knew, horror rising within me, that he would say something he shouldn't.

'Well what he did to Trudi was unforgiveable. We had to do something.'

'Of course you did.' She patted his hand.

After lunch we walked the streets of Alençon. Eventually Vanessa caught up with me as we walked around the Basilique. She pulled me to sit by her in a remote pew.

'So tell me the truth Trudi.' Her eyes roved my face.

I knew I could not go on prevaricating. I had to try and mitigate what had happened ten years before.

'After France, when Ellie was so possessive of me, and you used me, he knew what was going on. Stuart told me that he sat outside my bedroom in your villa and listened to Ellie making love to me. He also knew about Tom. He became obsessed. I was seeing a friend's older brother, Michael, occasionally and Stuart was very jealous. We went for a cycle ride into the country one Sunday, and he got me drunk. On the way home, we stopped to change into our school uniforms and he forced himself on me touching my breasts and they were so tender from the hormones. I slapped him. He lost his temper. He was so big and strong. It was not his fault. I am sorry.'

'No, there is more isn't there. He did more than……What did he do Trudi? I want to know.'

'Why Vanessa. I want to forget. It is over, a long time ago when we were different people.'

'Oh no Trudi. You are the same now as then, even though you are now beautiful and changed physically. He is the same. He has never got over you, I know. Whenever your name is mentioned he wants to know more but feigns indifference. I know my children. So tell me.'

'He wanted the same as Tom. If you can do it for that scumbag, you can do it for me, he said.'

'So, your pal Wally planted the marijuana. I suppose it was the best solution. And it all comes back to me, what I did to you.'

'I am sorry. I never wanted you to know.'

'I know you didn't Trudi, but you know, ever since you walked into our kitchen as a girl with Stuart that day, with your ears pierced with those little paste studs, I have suspected that he lied and you took the blame.'

'It is a long time ago. I am happy. I trust he is happy. He has two children and a nice wife. I saw her at the wedding. They looked like a couple.'

'Oh yes, I think they are happy enough. Sometimes it is impossible to know with Stuart. He is a bit of a lumpen oaf, a boorish farmer.'

'Vanessa, he was sixteen, full of hormones. I must have been, I mean my androgyny and change must have been very confusing for *him*, in fact I think I was the only one not confused by it. Everyone around me was confused *by* me.'

'I do not blame you at all Trudi. As you say, it was a long time ago. I am sorry for my part in it.'

'Vanessa, whatever your motives and whatever I did for you, I bear no grudge, I have no regrets. It was all part of my journey. When Simon died, it was as though the first part of my life was truly over. Oh yes I mourned him, I loved him, but he was part of my transition. All that early part of my life is over. I am mistress of Beauvonne and owner of a premier league fashion house. I have three children to raise and love, and my future studies to look forward to. My life is full. My cup, as the bible says, runneth over. I am happy. You set me on the road to happiness. I would ask you to think of your modelling career. You probably did a few things you didn't want to do. It is like the actresses who have posed nude or auditioned on the couch. Unfortunately, it is what we women have to do. But we survive. I love you Vanessa, otherwise I would not have invited you. Come let us find some sunshine and leave this ice cold church.'

We left the dull interior and emerged into strong warm sunshine. On the steps, she grasped both my hands and kissed me.

'I do wish you had been my child. I would have cherished you. Thank you for being so discreet and for your forbearance. I love you more than my own, except for Ellie. I am really proud of her. And I am proud of you, proud that in a small way, I could help you on your way.'

I bit back tears. So many emotions had been raised in our talk. All I could do was squeeze her hand. If I had tried to speak no words would have come out and I would have cried. I bent and picked Sébastien up, kissed him and jiggled him while I collected myself.

We walked back to the river as a party and I managed to have a few words with Wally. 'I told Vanessa about school. She knows the truth and I think, bears us no grudges. I will see you in the Maison tomorrow Wally. Thanks for everything.'

Chapter 19.

I was quite disturbed emotionally after my talk with Vanessa. I had spoken of things long dormant in my brain and best forgotten. At least I had not told of Stuart's savagery, nor his abandonment of me. I did not know what Vanessa would do, whether she would speak to Stuart about it or whether she could stow it away in the deep recesses of her mind, where many keep their infidelities, deceits, prejudices and nasty secrets. I can do that, but I know some can't. I have had to bury things, as a defence, as a means of just getting through this life. And I am happy. I would actually say, I am as happy as anyone. What I did to Stuart, to Dirty David the tennis coach and to Paul Morel, even playing Simon's mistress does not normally play on my conscience. Vanessa had disturbed my equilibrium.

That time ten years ago, when I was in suspended puberty, with drugs circulating through my veins holding back the dreadful effects of male development, had been exceptionally difficult. I had to hold on to the belief that whatever the mirror told me, when I appeared nude before it, I was really female. Every day I checked to make sure I was not developing male characteristics. Everyday in school, there would be someone trying to lift my skirt or squeezing a breast or just breathing 'pervert' as they passed by, and I had to have the strength to ignore it and maintain my dignity. I knew that to react was what the bullies wanted, so I denied them the pleasure. I remained aloof, remote, ignoring the puerile prejudice. Stuart had been part of that era.

Vanessa and I were up early to depart for Paris, leaving Sophie to come in with the children. As we left the Chateau, the children were breakfasting. We both kissed them all goodbye.

I always felt uneasy knowing that the children were on the road with someone other than me, but Sophie was a careful and reactive driver. I did not say be careful or any other such silly admonition, I had to trust her.

Vanessa was quiet on the ride. I left her to her thoughts and switched on the news. The latest casualties in Afghanistan had been announced and I was relieved that neither Harry nor Alison was named. I switched it off.

'I have to spend the morning in the office Vanessa. What do you want to do?'

'I will see a few old friends. They may even give me a few things.'

'Do you mean all day?'

'I expect someone will take me to lunch. You know Trudi, I quite envy you your life. Oh I know you have such dreadful difficulties, but you have seen life from all sides of the sexual spectrum. And ended up with Sabine, who clearly loves you.'

'There I am indeed fortunate. Sabine loves me for me, not for what I can give her. Simon gave me much, but there was a price to pay. Ellie seemed mostly to want me for sex, she found me irresistibly arousing, but my wishes took second place. Poor Stuart lusted, fascinated by a changeling. Sabine loves me, makes love to me, but I am always my own person, as she is her own. To find the perfect partner, and I think I have, is the most difficult trick we try to achieve. Even parents want something from their children, well, often they do. I only have one sorrow, my birth as a boy. Yes you are right. I am very fortunate and I appreciate all I have, money, loves, and an interesting life full of joy.

'Anyway have a good time with your contacts but if not, give me a ring and we will meet up. I thought today to take Nicole and Wally to lunch, a business meeting, but I can do that in the office this afternoon if *you* need company. The rest of the week I shall be mostly yours unless something happens. But start off in the Maison and see what we are at. It is very exciting.'

I showed her around. Nicole had neglected to tell me at the weekend that the lease had been signed for next door, and I found a doorway being made through and an architect with a plan in hand. I had given Nicole the barest outline of what I wanted and she had gone ahead without further consultation. At first I was annoyed, then I thought, if I am going to hand over the reins, then this was an opportunity to show some faith and delegate. Nicole, the architect and the builder formed a trio in the large top floor.

'Oh Trudi,' she said, 'let me introduce Albert Moreau, the architect and show you the plan.'

I shook hands and introduced myself. I glanced at the plan.

'It is your project Nicole, I am leaving it to you. You don't need my approval do you? You have thought of everything? Consulted with the designers? Plenty of room in the design suite for all our design team? Just one thing, we need glass in the windows that cannot be seen through from outside, yet lets plenty of light in. We cannot be too careful. I would like to have lunch with you and Wally. Shall we say one o'clock? I will book somewhere. I will tell Wally as you are occupied. À bientôt.'

We caught Wally in his office. Vanessa did not make eye contact with him. I could tell that she was finding the truth about Stuart very difficult. We went from there to my office.

Sometimes one has to face difficulties, in fact I always believe it is better to face them than let them fester below the surface. I needed to say something..

'About Stuart Vanessa. What he did was terrible. But it is in the past. I bear him no ill will. He was mesmerised by me, and he was just a teenage boy with rampant hormones coursing through his system. Don't be too hard on him, nor on yourself. And Wally only did what he did, to protect me.'

'I know, but it is hard for me to forgive Stuart. We tried to raise a gentleman but he has grown up a rude boor. You are charitable in excusing his behaviour Trudi, and you were in enough trouble. I don't know how you managed. Then Stuart! I am not upset with Wally, but I am ashamed.'

'I would like to think that you can put this to the back of your mind. I can assure you that I have. It was a pubescent thing, and your kindness and help has more than made up for ten such incidents. Vanessa, I owe you everything. All that I have stems from your reaction to me that first day and the subsequent holiday in France. You even found a Professor to give me the right drugs to prevent maleness. That is why you are here Vanessa, and why I have the deepest regard for you.'

'It is mutual Trudi.' We kissed.

'So what do you think of what we are doing? We used to be a little dress designer. We now do menswear, underwear, bags, perfume and are moving into stockings and cosmetics. Simon was the ultimate gentleman but he was not a man of vision.'

'Yes he was a gentleman, a true aristocrat and his manners have rubbed off on you. The way you have chosen your team and promoted from within. You learned a lot from him.'

'So much Vanessa. About food and wine, about France, horse riding, managing people. Toughness and yes, charity. I do still miss him, of course I do, but hard work, being busy does not allow time for endless grief and self-pity. When he died I was a mess. Eventually Nicole told me nicely to snap out of it, that Beauvonne needed me and she was right. It is only two years since Catherine died and we were in Clermont looking after Simon in hospital. My life seems like a whirlwind, with even the soil beneath my feet moving. A year ago, we married and toured Scotland for a honeymoon. That was a magical time and I did not even imagine life without him. Now I sleep with a woman who I also love and I am delegating everything to a young management team. Jacques is the father of the team at forty! Beauvonne and the Chateau and above all the children, they are stability. It is my aim to put Simon's legacy on a real firm substantial footing, not hand to mouth as it was under him and under his father. The estate under Sabine is looking immaculate, but more important, Sabine is a good farmer too. It is making more than twice as much money as when Simon managed it.

'And Maison Beauvonne will make money, for me and for the staff. I am going back to medicine. Simon wanted me to finish my studies and more importantly, I want to. It has always been my dream to cure people, for I know what suffering can be. Yet I have been so very lucky, blessed with a brain and looks, and through you all this. I sometimes have to just stop, look around me and make sure that it is not all a dream.'

'Oh your life is real enough Trudi and much of your success is just down to your character. I love you as my own. I can confess, now that you are a mature person with a life of your own, that I half hoped things would work out between you and Eleanor. It was very naughty of me, but I think you would have been so good for her, calmed her down. Oh well, that was just a silly dream.' She seized my hand and squeezed it. 'Now tonight, what are we going to do?'

'I thought I would see if there is a concert at La Madeleine, or the Opera. What would you like to do?'

'That would be lovely. Would you be able to get seats this late?'

'I am an A lister. It is a perk I seldom use, so I do not feel guilty. Of course I can get seats.'

'Then tomorrow I would like to eat out, on the Bateaux Mouches or that lovely little place in Montmartre or Willi's you told me about. My treat.'

'I will see what can be done. Do you have a posh frock for the opera?'

'Oh no, unless someone gives me one today.'

'I will see what is available, then phone you. Perhaps a friend will lend you a dress if necessary.'

Vanessa departed and I phoned for tickets. I took a box for Palais Garnier, where Simon and I had been just over a year ago. They had The Italian in Algiers playing. I phoned to tell Vanessa to borrow a dress. I booked Willi's bar for afterwards, so it was all within walking distance of the villa.

I spoke to Wally about lunch. Afterwards I did a tour of the Maison, speaking to as many as possible. I ended with the designers and they all seemed content and busy, even Thomas seemed to have forgiven Nicole. Nicole appeared at

12.30. I asked her to shut the door and pull up a chair next to me.

'How is it going with the alterations?'

'Oh fine Trudi. The gang start tomorrow. The Mairie approve the changes. I can get the plans if you like?'

'No Nicole, it is up to you. You are now in charge of Publicity. That includes of course, staging the shows. I would like to hear about plans for the next one and I may have some input, but after that it will be up to you. I am also making you Assistant MD. Jacques will be head of Design and Thomas his assistant. Wally is MD from henceforth. Is that clear?'

'Yes Trudi. I am only twenty-three. Are you sure my appointment will not alienate other people?'

'You know how to handle them, strength and diplomacy. Show you care and are efficient and they will respect you. They do already. Wally is overall in charge. He has a good brain, a cool head, and a presence, but I wonder whether he is very innovative?'

'Not as inventive as you, non. He has no flair but he is very efficient and a good salesman because people like him.'

'That is where you come in. As a pair I think you will work well together. You are my little sister Nicole and I adore you. I do not know how I would have survived since Simon died without you, and before, organising me. I trust you above anyone. This place has to make money. Everything must be costed. We can make a loss on some items provided we make it up on other lines. Liaise with the accountant, make her feel important, but judgement is yours. Keep an eye on the designers. Oh I trust Jacques to do a good job, but all the same. And this new salesman, he will need guidance. Wally will do that but you need to help too. He has to understand not only who we sell to but the ethos of Beauvonne, our public image and what we want that to be. And results, he must show results and that means profitable sales, not just volume. That is not your job, it is Wally's, but I look to you for staff morale, the listening and advising that you can give people.'

'Does this mean that you are leaving us?'

'I shall be around, but yes in three months I shall be studying again. I need to prepare myself. I shall work in this office, so I will be here if needed, but only if needed. You and Wally do what I used to do between you. Involve the office manager. You decide on venues for the shows, she will need to do the bookings and organising. You manage, but delegate the tasks. You understand Nicole? I am counting on you more than anyone, more than Wally even. But I feel his presence is needed to front up Beauvonne. You can wheel me out like a dummy at the shows and other events, and I will keep in touch. But I have confidence in you. If you ever have any doubts at all, then come and discuss things with me.'

'I will not let you down Trudi.'

'Good. I have a deep respect for you Nicole and love. Let's collect your beloved and go for lunch.'

I led the way to Fouquet's on the Champs. Nicole and Wally walked hand in hand. It was sweet to see.

We were shown to a secluded table where we could talk openly.

I went over the same information I had shared with Nicole.

He was shocked that I was withdrawing so soon.

'You knew it was coming. This way I am around for the next three months, accessible, but you will be running things, including the autumn shows. You have each other to count on, and a strong management team behind you. I have spoken to our dear accountant. We need to watch our costs but also have to maximise profits. I want you to make me rich, oh and yourselves too. You are both happy with these arrangements?'

'Oh yes Trudi. I am sure we can maximise on the ground you have laid.'

'Good. Thank you both. And you two, how is it.'

'We are in love Trudi.' Nicole said. 'Even this Englishman has said he loves me.'

'That is marvellous news. So are you going to marry?'

'Perhaps next year.'

'When you do, it is at the Chateau please. It will give me so much pleasure. And I am having more rooms renovated over the winter, more room for your families to stay. You will use the Chateau?'

Nicole said, 'We hoped you would offer.'

I was distracted as I saw Vanessa enter with Pierre on her arm. She wore a different dress from when she left me this morning. She was obviously working her magic.

'We are going to the opera tonight. Why don't you come? It is evening dress and I have a box. Please, to cement our future together?'

That evening, we met in the foyer of Palais Garnier. We had champagne and canapés sent to the box. Nicole wore a French blue dress that suited her blonde looks so wonderfully. I wore black, in respect for Simon, knowing that we would be photographed. Vanessa sparkled in sequined silver.

L'Italiana in Algeri was wonderful. Rossini's soaring themes and arias and of course the romance of the occasion. I had a period of sadness as I remembered my visit there with Simon, when he had dressed me so carefully to outshine anyone else. I held back my tears when thinking of him and studied the synopsis of the opera. It was completely bonkers, but then one seldom goes to the opera for the story. It is the music and the occasion that make the atmosphere. We all enjoyed it, helped by champagne and the most delicious canapés.

We walked in the warm evening air to Willi's. It was very lively, with several show business people there including an English group and their entourage. Strangely they were behaving themselves except for the odd guffaw. We settled at our table. Nicole and I exchanged glances, for this was where we had come the night Simon died. Everywhere I went in Paris, I was reminded of him with good memories of his love and care, and his education of me in the finer things in European culture, music, art and cuisine.

Vanessa had recovered from yesterday and the revelations of her son's behaviour. She was expansive, telling tales of her days as a model, dancing with Mick Jagger at a party, and of falling in love with him. Alas, but good for me, that infatuation had come to nothing or I would never have met her.

'I met Mick too Vanessa, on our honeymoon in Glasgow. He has still got it, just the way he looks at you.'

'I bet he has, It was always his mesmerising eyes.'

Wally too had revived, finding that his partial revelation had not coloured Vanessa's attitude to him. Nicole was gorgeous, lovelier than I had ever seen her. Her elfin features were set off in a new hairstyle, her blonde hair cut skilfully in a bob that made her small features even more exquisite. How fortunate I was to be in the company of these gorgeous and witty people.

'So how do you see the future of Beauvonne Wally?' Vanessa asked.

'Well the immediate future is one of consolidation Vanessa. We have expanded into so many new lines under Trudi's management, that we need time to refine and develop them. Trudi is a woman of vision, extraordinary imagination, but likes to delegate the detail. That is no criticism. A company needs an ideas person and people to attend to the detail. I can do the latter. Now we are costing everything. With haute couture, dealing with the fashionable rich, one made a dress and thought of a number. A gentleman's suit for a thousand euros, has to be costed carefully, cut without waste, the material has to be right and at the right price. There is a lot of work to do. Madame Trudi has ordered that we all make ourselves rich, so we have to work hard to that end.'

I was relieved to hear Wally make a really coherent reply, for we had not had this conversation. I realised that Vanessa had said it to provoke some sort of argument and perhaps to find a weakness. It was rather naughty.

She turned her attention to Nicole. 'And what do you do Nicole?'

'Now that is an interesting question,' I said before Nicole could answer, 'and she will tell you what her future is, but Nicole has been my right hand. She started off as my PA when Simon involved me in advertising and promotion. Through all the traumas of the past two years, Nicole has been there to guide and support me. I am lucky to have had such good friends around me and my dear friend Nicole, has been the best and amongst the most able. She will tell you what the future is though.'

'Trudi that is so sweet,' Vanessa said.

'I am quite embarrassed Vanessa, but I know that Trudi really means what she says. We are like sisters, yes, but she is the boss. I am now Marketing and PR director and as well as Deputy MD. As Wally says, we have plenty to do to take Beauvonne to the top. But Trudi has made it a family firm, we are all involved, with shares, and we love it and love her. We are committed Madame, to Beauvonne and to dear Trudi.'

'Now I know that Trudi is safe, with such committed lieutenants. I think you have chosen wisely Trudi. How very clever you are.'

'I have grown up in a hard school Vanessa. Life as you know was difficult. I did not grow up in a slum, but neither were we rich. My problems though, brought me much grief and isolation. I grew up suspicious of people so I let my head rule me. It so happens that along the way, I have found people I also love and who love me. If I do not gel with people, I leave them alone. If they attempt to hurt me, then I can be vicious, ruthless. Now I want to get back to medicine and leave the day to day running of Maison Beauvonne to my dear *lieutenants* as you call them. You think I have chosen well, but in a way, they have chosen me too. I have a super team here and at the Chateau.'

'Little Trudi. So grown up. When I think back....'

'Don't go there. In any case, Wally knows exactly what I was like.'

'I do know what you were like, Trudi. Before you changed, you were a strange creature, a sort of tomboy, mischievous, pretty, too pretty for a boy, dainty but wild. I confess that I liked you but was somewhat afraid of admitting it, because behind your back, well let's just say, questions were asked. Suddenly you became a lady, the best looking girl in the school, and I somehow understood. I too had grown up and was manly enough to show support and friendship. It was as though someone had waived a magic wand.'

'And that fairy godmother, waiving the wand was my dear friend Vanessa, she taught me so much, from what to wear and when to wear it, how to use makeup and how to walk in heels, as well as getting me the right medical attention. You three are, with Sophie and Sabine, the most important people in my life. If I talk anymore or think anymore about my past, I shall burst into tears. Tell me Vanessa, what are you doing for the rest of the summer?'

'Oh nothing very thrilling. We are having the usual fete for the village on a meadow and I have to arrange all that. And I have to play grandmother to Stuart's children, who I do love, but I find them so tiring. I have an appointment at hospital, a follow up to a routine breast screen, which is worrying, that is the week I return from here. Eleanor will come home, I hope. And Claire too, so life is full.'

I was too shocked to say anything. She was so matter of fact about her hospital appointment.

Nicole spoke first. 'Vanessa, I hope this hospital call is just a scare. It often is you know.'

'There is something there. I can feel it. But it could be benign of course. Thank you Nicole.'

'Vanessa. I too hope it is benign. You will let me know as soon as you hear, or perhaps you would like me to come to hospital with you? Of course, I could arrange for you to have the biopsy while you are here. What do you say?'

'That is sweet of you Trudi, but while I am here I just want to have a nice time with you. If you would come to hospital with me, it would be wonderful, but I feel it is asking too much. I shall be fine.'

'Have you told the children?'

'No not yet. I do not want to alarm them unnecessarily.'

'Then I will certainly come over Vanessa, of course I will. It is little to do for a dear friend. So what else would you like to do in Paris?'

'Just to be with you and see as much as I can.'

'Then why don't we get a Paris Pass and really do the City? It means no waiting in queues, bus fares paid, everything. And we can eat out at night. We'll do the Bateaux Mouches too, like real tourists. It will be such fun.'

'That sounds a brilliant plan Trudi. Thank you.'

Chapter 20.

We managed a fabulous week, whisking from one venue to another, seeing more art in a week than I had seen in my life. Simon could have told me everything about it, but I took the earphones and tried to absorb as much of the commentary as possible. Vanessa flitted, dismissing anything that didn't attract. She would disappear then return to drag me to see a picture that took her fancy. It was frustrating, when I was doing my best to assimilate as much knowledge as possible, trying to be a culture vulture. However, it was rewarding to see her enthusiasm in spite of her worries. Otherwise, she was the best companion, energetic, open eyed and fun loving. At fifty-five she had more energy than a teenager and with Wally minding the shop, I was allowed all the time needed to keep up with her whims. Of course, she also found time to visit old friends and collect 'pressies' as she called her freebees. We went to see Pierre again, who had fancied me when I was a boy girl and I had slept with him. He held my hand too long and I eventually wrenched it free, looking directly into his face. I smiled. 'Its been a long time,' I said, 'except for at Longchamps, when was that, three years ago?'

He smiled his most charming oily smile and it was like looking into the mouth of a crocodile. Of course he had indulged in paedophilia with me. At the time, I was not yet fifteen. I could bring a case against him, but he had paid me off with a complete wardrobe and look at me now. I am mentally intact, free to make whatever decision I like. I hovered while Pierre oiled over Vanessa, and I wondered what the tie was between them.

When we first met, Vanessa had seemed a remote aunty-like figure, kind but authoritative, the mother of my study companion. This week I had seemed the sober one and she the teenager. It was interesting meeting her fashion friends and seeing their reaction to Beauvonne. They were mostly very inquisitive but also complimentary. I knew several of them and it was useful to renew acquaintances in the trade. They were surprised when I told them I was returning to medicine. They thought me somewhat mad to turn my back on Beauvonne at a time of such development. I said that I had left a young, strong team to consolidate what I had put in place. They were most interested in our factory in Clermont Ferrand.

'Simon set up the factory and it was the best idea. At first it made a loss, but as we have added lines, the factory has grown and is nearing capacity. I am a believer in making European goods in Europe, rather than use the slave labour, sweat shops of the East. The conditions there are appalling as the latest disasters have shown. The advantages of manufacture in Europe are turn round times, a quarter of those making in the East, quality control and output is greater here which dilutes some of the added costs. But in a luxury market, which all our lines are, we can take a slightly higher on cost, because we have control over everything. I strongly recommend it. If things go well, we will open another factory here.' I said to Pierre when we met for dinner.

He raised his nicely trimmed eyebrows. 'And would you make for other fashion houses Madame?'

'Would you be interested Pierre?'

'I could be, not for high fashion of course, but for underwear or readymade.'

'Provided we have spare capacity, oui, bien sûr, je pourrais être. (I could be, of course). But Pierre, as you are an old friend of Simon and only for your kindness to me many years ago. I am not looking to make for all the fashion houses of Paris and beyond. I have no immediate plan for an expansion. We are too busy at the moment, working on our own range. I will remember this conversation though Pierre and perhaps next year we might work something out.'

The weekend was spent at the Chateau with the children. It was a happy time tinted with sadness. It was just a year since the helicopter had landed in the grounds to whisk Simon and I off on our honeymoon to Scotland. I was suddenly nostalgic for those drives through the mountains, misty mornings and curtains of distant rain, the smell of peat and cosy hotels.

Vanessa and I drove to Charles de Gaulle to take the plane for London. At Heathrow I hired a car and drove us with all Vanessa's added baggage of 'pressies' to the frightening, agoraphobia provoking, flat lands of her Lincolnshire.

We arrived at dusk, just as I had over 11 years before. At that time, I had an intense dissatisfaction with myself. Fourteen and a bit then, I had hardly known who or what I was. All I knew was that my body was not as it should be and I had to do things that I did not want to do and wear clothes that I hated. Above all, I craved the company of girls of my age, to be with, to play with and converse with and to copy. I identified with them yet could not be one with them. I saw them from afar and wanted to be them. Thinking back, I had been struggling in a nightmare while at school. Holidays were spent as a girl and I had my dear friend Heather to look after me but school was an imprisonment of my psyche as well as my body. Before returning to France, I resolved there and then to go and see dear Heather.

When I moved to France at eighteen, I was cut off from those old friends. It had been right for me to escape my past, but now I felt strong enough to revisit the pain of my childhood and youth. I had even wanted to escape my parents, father who sent me away to boarding school in a desperate effort to help me find masculinity and mother, who though indulging my desires also displayed disappointment and voiced it within my hearing.

The farmhouse was hardly changed from my remembrances of it. Vanessa's husband, John, stood up as we entered, kissed her and then surprisingly kissed me too. I felt slightly embarrassed. It was the first time I felt he really accepted me. When it was discovered by them, so long ago now, that I had cross dressed and in his elder daughter's clothes, he had been so angry. It was Vanessa who had taken control, and dressed me provocatively to trap Tom. She had used me. John had washed his hands of me.

Vanessa immediately launched into a review of her two weeks with me. Her effusive praise and delight was wonderful but slightly embarrassing. At length John said, 'I'll take Trudi up to her room, then I'll come back for your bags. There's cold meat and salad in the fridge Vanessa.'

I was shown to the same room I had occupied on every visit. 'When you are ready, come down for supper. I just want to say Trudi, thank you for looking after her and thank you for coming home with her. It is very kind of you to take so much trouble. You and I have not been on good terms. I am afraid I did not understand your syndrome, but I have to say you have earned my respect.'

'I said I would go to hospital with her John, because I love her. She has been so good to me, it is the least I can do and I will know the right questions to ask the consultant.'

'What do you think they will find?'

'I don't know. The consultant may know after they have done a scan. But they will probably do a biopsy too. It may be some days before we have an answer. If it is cancer, and if it is caught early enough, the outlook could be positive. It is no good anticipating anything John. We just have to be patient. Are you coming to the hospital?'

'I don't know. I hate those places.'

'I think you should, at least to sit and wait outside the consultants room. Vanessa is being very brave, but it must be a great worry.'

'I know. In truth, I am a bit of a coward over this. I find it quite daunting. I am eight years older than Vanessa. It should be me that is sick. It seems all wrong that my lovely wife should be ill.'

'That is precisely why you need to give her support John, isn't it? I shall be there to take the strain and any tears, though I don't think Vanessa will shed a tear. More likely I will.'

'You are right. I will come, at least as far as the door.'

'Good. You better go down. I just want to freshen up.'

I unpacked a few things and used the en suite. I sat on the loo and suddenly tears burst forth. I sobbed quietly. It seemed as though a chapter of my life was closing. I pulled myself together, repaired my make up, pinched my cheeks and went down. Vanessa had laid the table with the contents of the fridge, thoughtfully bought in by John. Half lobsters, dressed crabs, some ham and beef, salads bought from an upmarket supermarket and wine. It was a feast.

We chatted about our two weeks and Vanessa showed John her snaps on her camera. We had just finished when the back door opened and Ellie appeared silhouetted against the brightness of the yard light. As the door closed I could see her clearly. She was bronzed, yet there were dark semi-circles below her eyes and creases in her forehead. She had aged ten or so years since those first crazy days in Paris.

She flung her arms around her mother and kissed her hard, then turned to her dad.

Lastly, she came around the table to me and I stood, as tall as her in my heels. She clasped me to her, rocked back from our touching stomachs and looked hard into my face with her piercing eyes.

'So little Trudi. It is nice to have you here, especially at this time. No, more than that, I have never been more pleased to see anyone.' She kissed me hard on the lips and parted, still holding onto my hand.

'I say mother,' she said, 'look at this woman. Isn't she perfect? Her little nails and perfect skin. You did a good job on her mother.'

'I am very proud of her,' Vanessa said, 'but I merely set her on the right road.'

'Where have you come from Ellie?' I asked to deflect attention.

'Africa,' she said, imitating the way Africans pronounced the name of that troubled and savage continent. 'You name it and I have probably been there. Libya, Tunisia, Mali, Nigeria Somalia, Egypt and a few others. I now have six months off and I need it. I am exhausted.'

We stayed at the table while she told of her adventures. She picked at the food. Eventually she said, 'I'm sorry. If I am to be of any use tomorrow, I have to go to bed. I'll see you in the morning.'

John, Vanessa and I sat and chatted for a little while, then I excused myself and went up. I found Ellie in my bed. There was a note on my PJs. 'I just want to feel your body next to me, nothing else.'

I went to the bathroom and removed my makeup. I slipped into bed, bumping against her, but she did not rouse. I was asleep quickly and slept soundly. I awoke to find her arm around my waist. I turned slowly to look at her. Her face was more relaxed than last evening, but the signs of strain were still there. I left the bed gently and took my clothing into the bathroom. I showered, dried my hair and dressed, did my makeup and returned to the bedroom. She still hadn't stirred.

I heard movement downstairs and descended to find Vanessa in the kitchen. John was already out on the farm.

'Is Ellie in your bed?' she asked.

'She was there when I went up last night. She had left a note on my PJs just saying she wanted to be next to me. I thought about it Vanessa and decided that it didn't matter. She was out on her feet. I thought we could give her breakfast in bed. What do you think? What would she like?'

'As long as she is not being a pest.'

'I am with Sabine, and much as I love Ellie, I will not be unfaithful. In any case, I do not want to lead her on. I want to be kind though.'

'Kind but firm Trudi. Well, toast, poached eggs and bacon and she loves fried tomatoes. Orange juice and coffee.'

We busied ourselves and loaded a tray. Vanessa shook her awake. She woke quickly once roused from slumber. She ran to the loo and returned to sit propped up while we plied her with food.

'Scrumptious,' she said as she finished the food and I poured her coffee. 'That was so good. So nice to be spoiled. Now mum, what time is the hospital?'

'Two-thirty, so there's no hurry. Anyway Eleanor, why are you in Trudi's room? I hope you are not being a nuisance.'

'I would be if she would let me, Mother. I just wanted to be near a human again. Unfortunately I slept like a log.'

'Just behave Eleanor. Trudi can't do with complications. She is with Sabine now.'

'Oh mother, I was just joking. I regard Trudi as my sister now. Anyway Trudi didn't object. She didn't have to get into bed.'

'Eleanor, don't be silly, what choice did she have. Tonight you will be in your own room. I can't do with your silliness. Trudi is too much of a lady to complain and you might do well to emulate her.'

'It was one night when I was dog-tired. I just wanted some comfort, some contact with a fellow human. I respect her, mother. Let's not start with a quarrel. You can't do with it and neither can I.'

Unexpectedly, she burst into tears. I could see how exhausted and emotionally bereft she was. I took the empty tray from the bed. I sat beside her and clasped her to me. I stroked her hair.

'You need rest and some love and care. Stay in bed, I'll take care of everything.' I drew the covers up and tucked her in, kissed her cheek as though she was one of the children.

In the kitchen, clearing the breakfast things, Vanessa said, 'Thank you Trudi for being so forgiving but be careful. Make no mistake, she still has the hots for you and she will take advantage.'

'I felt so sorry for her. She looks completely drained.'

'Oh I have no doubt of that. She endures terrible hardships in order to get an exclusive, but when it comes to you Trudi, she is obsessed. Be very careful not to let your natural caring instincts be deceived by her. She can turn it on when she wants. I think that is how she gets out of scrapes abroad. She had an interview with a leader of Boko Haram, causing all the trouble in Nigeria, and managed to get away.

Consequently the Nigerian Government has banned her. She is so manipulative.'

'Well I am stronger too, Vanessa. Life is complicated enough without a lesbian affair.'

As I spoke the door opened and John walked in. 'Eleanor is awake I take it?' he said. 'Where did we go wrong raising our children?'

'Oh John, they are all right. Eleanor's lesbianism is not down to us. Claire is a swot, but I expect her to lead a normal and successful life and Stuart is on the farm with a wife and two children. Ellie is very successful in her career, don't forget that.'

I interrupted. 'Enough, I am an adult and I can handle Eleanor. We have other things to think about today. We should leave here at what time for the hospital, remembering that parking may be difficult?'

'If we leave at twelve-thirty it will be plenty of time.' John said.

Eleanor arrived downstairs late in the morning. She was subdued, and slightly disagreeable. 'I moved into my room,' she said tersely.

'Yes Ellie, I think that is for the best. You know my position.'

'You're no fun anymore Trudi. Too much the lady.' She said.

I ignored the remark, but I thought about it. Yes, I had become a serious person over the years. It was only Sabine who teased me and made me laugh now. I supposed that many, even Nicole and Wally were a bit in awe. I was after all, their boss, and a good many serious events had occurred. I had lost contact with my student friends. Élise and Jean Luc had moved out of the villa, and I had not seen them for sometime. This last year especially had been a serious time. Simon had been kind, exceedingly kind to me, but we had not laughed a lot. There had been so many swords of Damocles hanging over us. Catherine's death, Simon's amputation and the state of his heart and the children, had all been great worries, especially with the police investigating and I felt, watching every move.

Oh we were happy, working for and supporting each other, but we did not laugh. I think Simon was frightened to tease in case I took offence, knowing my frailties of self worth. He had done much to instil self-confidence. Making me the face of Beauvonne, putting me on the catwalk, horse riding, his little lectures on food, wine and the arts, had all helped at least with my visible persona. Inside, my birth as a boy still hurt and it always would, however thick the veneer of femininity became. And yet I knew how lucky I was. And I owed it all to Vanessa and to Simon, but especially Vanessa who had, for whatever reasons, taken me up as her project to become a great lady.

I wanted to be a great lady, above all things. I compared myself to David Beckham. He had been born to humble parents. He had also committed the unforgivable sin, of being sent off while playing for England, for a senseless foul. Fifteen years later, he was established as a gentleman, mixing with the upper echelons of society, with an OBE. My past was harder to live down, people forgave my accident of birth less readily than the deliberate actions of a silly young footballer. If I could at least have people's respect, I would be happy and I believed, I earned that from hard work, good manners and by making good decisions.

Our journey to hospital through the flat monotonous scenery of Lincolnshire, was uneventful, but did nothing to raise my spirits and draw me out from my introspection.

The hospital was new. It was light and airy but did not have the feeling of permanence of the old buildings I was used to. We found our way easily to the department and I shoved the appointment letter into the reader. It registered that Vanessa had arrived.

We sat waiting. No one in the reception area seemed able to speak. People in white coats or uniform appeared, called a name and patients followed to whatever fate awaited them.

Eventually her name was called. I remained seated as Vanessa rose from her chair. 'Trudi, I want you to come with me. John will stay here with Eleanor.'

I was perplexed I was going to demur, but Ellie waved me away. John sat reading an old magazine. I followed Vanessa into a tiny room in which a consultant and a nurse and the two of us barely fitted.

It was a brief interview. The consultant got straight to the point. They would do a biopsy tomorrow, but he suspected the worst from the scan. Following the biopsy, they would operate. From the size of the growth, a lumpectomy would not be appropriate, so the whole breast would be removed, and he suggested that it might be wise, given her DNA, to remove the second breast. If it proved malignant, then there would be radiotherapy and chemotherapy. He outlined what that involved emphasising that it was now much more effective and targeted.

Vanessa shook his hand and we left. We had been in the room no more than ten minutes. Outside Vanessa took me away from the waiting area.

'Trudi, I do not want Ellie and John to know that this may be serious, so play it down. If they go round with long faces, I shall not be able to bear it. It looks as though there is no alternative but to lose both breasts. The question remains, reconstruction or not. And if reconstruction, implants or my own tissue. Quite honestly I don't relish either. I don't have much spare tissue on my frame. Having foreign substances in my body also worries me. What do you think?'

'If I were you I would not want surgery on another part of my body as well as both breasts. Personally I would have the implants. Thousands have had them, so they are tried and tested, especially after the last scare, but it is how you feel. Some people don't miss their breasts and don't have reconstruction. I would have reconstruction but I cannot decide for you.'

'No but your clever mind has put all the alternatives. I think implants Trudi and as for the rest of the treatments, I will just have to face it.'

'You will have to tell your girls because if they have inherited this defective gene, they may have to consider preventive surgery.'

'Ellie would not mind I think, but Claire, that could be a different matter. She has had several boyfriends and once university is out of the way and she has a career, she may have babies. We had better find Ellie and John and go home. Thank you for being my sounding board Trudi.' We kissed.

On the way home, we were quite silent. I don't think anyone, well Eleanor or John knew what to say and dared not ask for fear of getting the wrong answer.

As we neared the farm, Eleanor said, 'Tonight I have booked the Theatre, light and fluffy, Jersey Nights, about Frankie Valli and the Four Seasons and a restaurant after. So we need to get our glad rags on and be prepared for a sing along.'

'Oh thank you Ellie,' Vanessa, replied, 'that will certainly amuse John and I. Do you know who they are Trudi?'

'I have heard of them, so I expect when they start I shall recognise the songs. It sounds a great night Ellie, thank you.'

'And I am paying mum, my treat.'

'That's very thoughtful Eleanor, but you really didn't have to.'

'But I wanted to mother.'

I realised that Eleanor was really very fond of her mother. Perhaps she had deeper feelings for people than I had seen. It occurred to me that she disguised her emotions with the outrageous behaviour and over the top responses.

I sat quietly. It was great to have something to amuse us rather than to go home and slob out in front of TV with all the horrible worrying thoughts racing through our minds.

In my bedroom sorting out what to wear from my suitcase, I was interrupted by Ellie sliding in the door.

'So what did they say Trudi.'

'Have you asked Vanessa?'

'No, I can't. It's too horrible.'

'Well you will have to talk to her, won't you. Come and sit on the bed with me Ellie.' I told her what had been said, and tried to speculate about what would happen, putting it as gently as one can about such news. I also said that of course, until the biopsy, nothing was certain, so it could be better news, a little sugar on the pill. It did not soothe her.

'God this is awful. Poor mum, and I have been such an annoyance to her over the years.'

'She loves you Ellie. She accepts you and your provocative actions and sometimes thoughtlessness. She doesn't think any the less of you. She admires that you do and say things without pretence and she respects your career and your bravery. Both of us, would not do what you do, for one thing, what would we do if we could not plug the hairdryer in? Now she needs your gentle support. We just have to hope for a good outcome.

'There is something though Ellie, and I am sure Vanessa will not mind if I tell you. Vanessa has a defective gene making breast cancer a greater than average possibility. You need, and so does Claire, to get it checked out and see whether you have it too.'

'And if we have it?'

'They will give you the options Ellie. You know what Angelina Jolie has done? That is one option, but there are other alternatives.'

'Thank you doctor Trudi. It's a lot to think about.'

'I'm afraid it is Ellie.' I kissed her and held her hand. 'Will you tell John or would you like me to? And of course Stuart too.'

'I am the eldest, it is my duty.' She left me.

I dressed in one of the two dresses I had brought. I spent time titivating and lingering in the privacy of my room. I phoned Nicole and told her what was happening and where I was. Everything was under control at the Maison, she said. I wished Vanessa a speedy recovery. I phoned Sabine and told her what was happening and that I would return in two days' time.

'I'm missing you,' she said, 'but do not worry. All is well here. The children are all well and Sophie and Laurent too. You do what you have to do for your friend.'

'I love you Sabine.' I said. And put the phone down. Had I said that before? I could not remember, actually declaring myself so openly. I think I had said coolly, that we would give it a go, or words to that effect. Faced with another crisis in what I considered my family, I had subconsciously declared myself. As I recognised at last that it was true, I did love her, I felt quite elated. The future suddenly seemed clearer and more concrete.

My phone rang. 'Je t'aime, ma chère Trudi.' I heard Sabine say, then the line went dead.

I found everyone dressed and when I finally descended to the living room. 'Everything is well in France,' I said brightly. 'The children and the Chateau and of course Maison Beauvonne. Nicole has control as Wally is in the US. She is a safe pair of hands just as Sabine is at the Chateau. It is a relief that I do not have to think of everything now. Are we all ready?'

'Yes we should go,' Vanessa said, 'we can get chocolates on the way.'

The theatre was packed, mostly older people and I wondered what was coming. When the curtain went up, we were presented with a 1950s type bar and a minor concert. A narrative was given of the Jersey boys and a history of their music, much of which I knew even if I had not known the singers. The audience participated and as the show went on, became ever more vociferous, singing along and clapping. By the end, everyone, even John stood up and swayed to the music. I saw that John and Ellie had an arm around Vanessa, Ellie's other arm around my waist. She turned and kissed her mother's cheek and then somehow found my lips for a quick kiss.

Afterwards we went to the Jew's House Restaurant. It proved a tranquil venue with some excellent dishes. We were home by eleven thirty and straight to bed.

Ellie knocked my door and surprisingly waited for my answer. 'Can I sleep with you,' she said, 'I need a cuddle. I won't do anything I promise.'

'And you mean that this time Ellie? OK but if you are not good, I will kick you out.'

'Promise,' she said, and for once, she kept her word.

Next day, Ellie and I drove to the hospital with Vanessa for the biopsy. We were told that she would be away three hours, so we took a bus to town and ate a snack in a small café. Eleven years ago I had walked these streets with Stuart, that day of my sort of 'coming out'. It was unbelievable how my life had changed since that day of such highs and lows.

We returned to hospital and found Vanessa had been admitted. They wanted to do a full scan and regardless of the result, said they would do a double mastectomy the day after. We found her in good spirits, but very sore. I looked at her, all makeup removed and suddenly so much older than two days ago when she was still my ex-model fairy- godmother. It was difficult for me not to cry. I asked whether there was anything I could get her from the small shop?

'Nothing. I have my magazines Trudi and I want to read all about you. I have been keeping this long article they did in OK, for a time when I had the time. So, off you two go and don't worry, I am fine. Just promise you will visit tomorrow after my op. And Eleanor, be good, you know what I mean.'

'Yes mother, of course.'

We kissed and left her after some feeble protests that we wanted to stay. She said she was tired and we should go.

On the way home I asked whether she had spoken to Stuart?

'No, not yet. I thought to go there now, on our way home if that is OK with you, and you would be there to back me up. I know you don't like Stuart but can you?'

'Yes of course.'

'What did go wrong there?'

'It's a long time ago Eleanor.'

'Eleanor! You only call me that when you want to repulse my advances. So he did something, didn't he? Did he try it on and you wouldn't let him. That was it wasn't it.'

'Don't rake up old ashes Ellie. We fell out at school, for various reasons. Yes, he could not come to terms with my change. He was infatuated and also a bit spiteful when I refused him. He was a confused teenage boy with too many hormones in a mostly male environment. It is in the past as far as I am concerned.'

Stuart's house was an ivy clad 17th century farmhouse, dark red brick and thatched roof. A Jaguar stood beside the porticoed doorway.

'Looks like he is in.' Ellie said.

Chapter 21.

Stuart certainly was in. He answered the door and stood almost filling the doorframe. I could not understand how he had become so large. When I had last seen him, he was sixteen and a bit. He was a big lad then, now he was a giant. In his last two years of growth he must have put on a terrific spurt of growth.

'Well, well, Trudi Nash. What brings you two here?'

'I need to talk to you about mother,' Ellie said, 'Trudi came over to see her.'

'Come in then. Put wood in the hole. Come into the kitchen. Tea or coffee?'

'Coffee please Stuart.' We both said.

'I can just about do that. Jenny is out so I am baby sitting. It's nice to see you again Trudi and you have become such a star. Always in the news."

'Not always for the right reason Stuart. How are you? You look well and a family man too.'

'Yes we are all OK. Busy on the farm, dad takes a bit of a back seat, doing the books and planning, but I do all the day to day management.'

'Stuart, I need to talk to you about mum. She is in hospital having an operation.'

'What for? Has she had an accident?'

'A double mastectomy Stu. Cancer. It has all been a bit sudden, that is why Trudi came back with her from France. They are operating tomorrow.' Ellie told him the ward and the phone number.

'She'll be OK though, won't she?'

'It will be a long job Stuart. When she has recovered from the operation there will be chemo and or radio therapy. With that comes susceptibility to contract illness because her resistance is greatly lowered. It will not be wise therefore for her to baby sit for fear of catching a bug from your children. She should just not make herself available.

'So it's really serious then Trudi. Is that your advice as a doctor?'

'I am not a doctor yet, but I have worked in oncology, so I know a bit about it, at least how they treat it in France.'

'So how long will she be considered at risk?'

'For at least six months, but over the next year too, her resistance to disease will be low. The therapy reduces her antibodies.'

'How is she?'

'You know mum. Is she ever down? She is brave Stuart, and she will be, but she needs our support. So don't think you will just be able to dump your kids on her as you have in the past.'

'No, I see that sis. We'll make other arrangements. So are you two together now?'

'No Stuart, we are not.'

'I suppose you are all right now you are a widow.'

'I miss Simon Stuart, if that is what you mean, and I have friends and for the time being a partner. But after Simon died, I was a mess and I gave up study for a year. I am shortly going back to my studies, but I also have a business to run, the estate and three little children to consider. All in all, my life must be a great deal more complicated than yours. Anyway, I am here tomorrow and then return to France.'

'You sound French. I like the accent. Very attractive. I understand that Wally works for you. Is he your partner Trudi?'

'No Stuart he is engaged to a friend of mine who also works for me. It has been nice to see you again. I don't know about Ellie but I am tired.'

'Yes so am I Trudi. Thanks for the coffee Stu. I will let you know how she is tomorrow and then perhaps you will visit? Don't let her down.'

'I'll visit Ellie,' he said as we went out of the door. 'Looking good Trudi.'

I made no reply. On the way home Ellie said, 'You really don't like him do you, I could tell. You are so transparent Trudi.'

'No, he has not improved with age Ellie.'

'He did something bad didn't he. And you got him expelled.'

'I don't think he was expelled as such, just asked to leave. It was drugs Ellie, nothing to do with me, not that I think he was taking. I just thought he was holding them for someone else.'

'Mmm. I think there is something else, but never mind. As you say, it is old ashes. You won't need to see him again.'

'Oh, well I hope he gives his mother some consideration.'

We ate spaghetti Bolognese with John and I went to bed soon after. I lay still and tired though I was, I could not sleep, my mind was full of Vanessa and of Stuart. Stuart was a slob. I realised that I had formed an intense dislike of him in those few minutes at his house. Meeting him again had unsettled me. In my unorthodox life, I had learned to control my emotions, but meeting the person who had raped me, even after all these years, was really strange. I had slept, had intercourse with a number of people, sometimes really against my wishes. But Stuart's rape had been entirely different. I realised suddenly the horror of it and why victims sometimes became so traumatised. All these years since the rape, I had felt guilty that I had been instrumental in his being expelled. But seeing him again, I found him unrepentant, with an underlying lasciviousness to his speech. I no longer felt any guilt. He had deserved punishment, but in the event, I had given him exactly what he wanted, agricultural college. I felt slightly cheated.

If Vanessa should die, it would be like losing my own mother. Ellie did not come to my room. In desperation I took half a sleeping pill and slept well, not waking until after seven. I lay thinking about the day ahead. I looked forward to returning to France, to the children and Sabine, from the gloom of the flat lands of Lincolnshire and the grave outlook it seemed for Vanessa.

I awoke bleary eyed and instead of lying thinking, immediately left my bed and showered. I dressed in my sunniest dress, light blue silk dupion, spent half an hour doing my hair, making it neat and tidy, up with ringlets at the back with no escaping wisps.

I went down alone to find John already breakfasting, looking every inch the country landowner in tweed jacket. I remembered my honeymoon and looking at the tweeds with Simon. Happy days.

'You're coming to the hospital John?'

'Of course, hate them, the smell is enough to put me off, but Vanessa is still my darling and I will do all I can to see her through this. Thank you for being here. It would have been even more gloomy without you and you know, Vanessa dotes on you.'

'Really?'

'You know that, don't you?'

'I thought she was just being very kind, that I was a sort of project perhaps.'

'Ah yes. Well that is how it started but we now think of you as one of ours. It has been useful to have your input on her illness too and she has very much valued your support. You are still going tomorrow?'

'I have to. There are things that need my attention, the business and the estate. Oh yes I have good people managing, but I have to keep an eye on what happens. Most of all, it is the children. I go back to hospital in three months and I will not see so much of them, so this is my time to bond.

'I hope that we will get some answers today, to take away the uncertainty, and of course I hope it will be good news. And I am a phone call away, if necessary I will fly over. I love Vanessa as my own mother, my fairy godmother.' I stopped, overcome by my emotions.

'You are a good girl Trudi and you are one of this family too. Thank you for all you have done.'

'Look, I know you don't like to leave the farm, but you have Stuart to look after it, and you have your villa in France. Why don't you come over in the autumn? Better still, come over and stay in my Paris villa. Vanessa loves it so and it would be a great place for her to recover. She has so many contacts and just loves the place.'

'It's a great idea Trudi. Thank you. I was vaguely thinking I should take her away, but I am, have been sort of wedded to the farm. It has always come first, so I have hardly stayed a week in our villa all the years we have had it. I will take her away. You are right.'

We heard that Vanessa was back on the ward just after five. John drove us to the hospital. We made our way with faint hearts to the ward, wondering what we would hear.

I spoke to the charge nurse at her desk.

'You are the family?'

'Yes, this is her husband and we are her daughters.'

'Would you take a seat and I will see if I can contact the consultant.'

We sat, not daring to speak to each other. The nurse returned after ten minutes.

'He is on the wards at the moment and will be with you shortly.' she said.

Time seemed to drag. Ten minutes went by then another seven. I watched as a man in his forties walked towards us, hoping that this was him, but he turned off and reappeared pushing a trolley.

More time passed. I hardly liked to look at my watch. Suddenly he was there. He asked us into a tiny office.

When we were seated, he smiled. 'I have good news. The biopsy shows no malignancy, so there is no danger of spread. We have removed the breasts and in the circumstances looking at her genetics, that was the right course of action. We will keep her in for two or three days and then we do not expect her to have any more problem.'

Ellie flung her arms around me and then hugged her father. John shook the consultant's hand and we exited to go to the ward. It was a terrific relief.

We found Vanessa propped on pillows. She looked so much older without her makeup but she offered a smile. 'Good news,' she whispered.

'Yes,' we said, 'very good news.'

Ellie sat and took one hand and John kissed Vanessa, then stood like a spare part.

'Trudi,' Vanessa said, 'come here dear.'

We kissed. 'I am so pleased,' I said. 'It is great news. Vanessa I could not be more pleased.'

Suddenly my throat constricted, and I could not speak. I wanted to sob with relief and with the knowledge that Vanessa truly loved her little changeling. I bit my lip and my breast heaved as I gave way, tears rolling down my cheeks.

We three women, our heads together, all crying, clung until Vanessa said, There, there, I am OK my darlings. Dry your tears. And Trudi, repair your face before you leave here.'

I found my mirror and wiped the tear stains away.

'Now you will have to get away for a good holiday, somewhere sunny and warm. I have suggested coming to the Paris villa, you and John, if you would like to, but maybe sunny and warm would be better. Some tropical paradise perhaps. I have a customer on Mustique, I will see what can be done. And by Christmas you should feel fit again, so come to the Chateau, all of you and then to Courchevel to ski.'

We stayed for half an hour. She was tired and asked us to go.

'I leave in the morning Vanessa. Ring me when you can. I love you.'

Next morning I said my goodbyes to John and Ellie and drove to my parents. I took them to lunch and decide to stay overnight so I could see Heather.

I took Heather out to the local pub. She was still at home with her mother, her boyfriend would not name the day and she would not move in with him until he did.

'What an old fashioned girl you are,' I said, 'I admire you for that.'

'Well sister Trudi, if he cannot give that much commitment then he doesn't want me that much. And you, now you are a widow?

'Oh do you remember Sabine?' I felt myself blushing. 'We are living together.'

'And?'

'Yes Heather, we love each other.'

'My dear little Trudi, you were blushing like when I first dressed you and painted your nails. I am happy for you.'

'Thank you Heather. Gosh that was a long time ago. How kind you were to me, my big sister.'

'I enjoyed doing it. It was so funny, dressing a boy as a girl.'

'Oh but you did it kindly.'

'Yes, but it was supposed to be a punishment. It was not until after that I realised that it was really what you wanted. Then I began to love you Trudi and I still do.'

'And I you Heather. I hope things work out for you. You must come and stay with us in Paris sometime.'

I returned to France in the morning. I slept all the way to Paris, missing the lunch and wine. I awoke as we pulled into Gare du Nord. I took a taxi to the mansion and was just in time to bath the children and tuck them up. I rang Nicole.

'I am back Nicole. Is there anything I should know?'

'No Trudi everything is fine. How is Vanessa?'

'It is good news. Non-malignant, but a double mastectomy, just in case. But a great relief.'

'I am so glad for you and of course Vanessa and her family.'

'Thank you Nicole. Is Wally home?'

'No, LA He will be back on Friday.'

'Are you available tonight?'

'What do you have in mind Trudi?'

'I thought Sophie and you and I could go out to dinner but only if you like.'

'Excellent idea. Who will baby sit?'

'Madame Gameau, I hope. I have to ask her. I will ring you back.'

We went to 'Autour de Midi', a jazz bar in Montmartre. They rolled out the red carpet for me, and we had an excellent evening. It was a relief after the emotional tension of the last few days.

Chapter 22.

I went home to the Chateau. Life was tranquil. I phoned Vanessa every other day, just to hear her voice and to be reassured that all was well.

I fell into a routine. Rise early, ride with Sabine if she was available, or Nicole if she was there or with Sophie once or twice when Laurent could baby sit. Sometimes I was back riding alone, my confidence restored. Tasha was always at our heels. At ten I would have a plate of porridge and play with the children, teaching them to read and count and even subtraction. They learned their tables too. In the afternoon we would try to do something exciting.

In the forest I had a treetop course installed and Nicole and I took them on it one by one, even Sébastien, and they soon overcame their fear. They loved the zip wire. When weather permitted we would swim, but I was tired of the outside pool. This winter they were installing a sliding canopy, which would roll back at the touch of a button, then it could be used all year and would not collect leaves dust and detritus.

I had a letter from the University, reminding me that my special leave was coming to an end. I was asked to confirm that I would resume my course in six weeks time.

I replied that I would and was pleased to find a week later that I was going back to Emergency under dear M. Deraveau.

I went to the Maison once a week. The Autumn show was huge, held at L'Olympia, and crammed with every celeb and buyer we could find as well as all the press. I modelled three dresses, saying that it would probably be for the last time. My first was a readymade, a brilliant little suit in a really pretty grey with a tinge of purple, called violet white. The dye was natural, made from heather. It was made of tweed, the finest material they could weave in that factory on the Isle of Harris. It was perfectly tailored to fit my figure exactly and lined with a close woven silver silk. The shop price I was told, would be €1,500 but it would be worth every penny. It was a tribute to Simon and my honeymoon. I wished Simon had been there to see it.

The second dress was classic black, full length, sleek, art nouveau retro, with black tubular sequins.

The last of course was a reference back, a tribute to Simon, my actual wedding dress. I was last on the catwalk with it and Wally who gave the commentary explained the relevance. Tasha raced on to be with me as I adopted a low curtsey at the end and the roof came off.

The gathering afterwards was wonderful, full of praise for the whole collection, and Wally had set up six desks staffed by our own people to take orders. The three great London stores all fought for the rights to buy certain designs and somehow it was sorted out which they would each have and which they would share.

We held the party that night. La Poulette who had modelled earlier, said she had never seen such a commercially successful show. I finally went to bed at five am.

The next month was spent revising my medical knowledge and with the children and riding.

Sabine had proved a wonderful support and a tender lover. The black shadow of dear Simon's death gradually faded. One day I dismounted from Sheba in my favourite glade where late autumn sunshine filtered through thinning leaves. Sheba munched the grass, her bridle and bit chinking. I sat on a log that I had asked to be left as a seat. It had been carved out with a chain saw and smoothed off.

I am not a spiritual person, but somehow I seemed to see Simon and he was smiling at me. I could almost feel his arm about my waist and hand across my diaphragm. I knew that he would have approved of what I was doing and even of my partnership with Sabine.

I decided then, that Sabine was ideal for me. I would ask her to become my legal partner. With Sabine there was none of the oppression of Ellie, the using of Vanessa or the kinkiness of Simon. I was fully content at last. Sister Sledge played in my head, 'Thinking of You'

I'm thinking of you and the things you do to me

That makes me love you, now I'm living in ecstasy.

Hey, it's you and the things you do to me

That makes me love you, now I'm living in ecstasy

I'm in love again, And it feels so, so good.

Made in the USA
Charleston, SC
28 July 2013